Dead Letter

Dead Letter

A Murder Mystery

Frank Shima

Beaver's Pond Press, Inc.

Edina, Minnesota

ISBN 10: 1-59298-245-X
ISBN 13: 978-1-59298-245-5

Library of Congress Control Number: 2008930976
Printed in the United States of America
First Printing: July 2008
12 11 10 09 08   6 5 4 3 2 1

Cover and interior design by Clay Schotzko
Cover illustration by LouAnn Hoppe

Beaver's Pond Press, Inc.

Beaver's Pond Press is an imprint of
Beaver's Pond Group
7104 Ohms Lane
Edina, MN 55439-2129
(952) 829-8818
www.BeaversPondPress.com

To order, visit www.BookHouseFulfillment.com
or call (800) 901-3480. Reseller discounts available.

This is a work of fiction. Names, characters, places, and incidents are the product of the author's imagination or are used fictitiously. Any resemblance to actual events or persons, living or dead, is entirely coincidental.

Dedication

*This book is dedicated to my brother, Ron,
who passed away in January of 2008.*

*Frank enjoying a summer afternoon and
looking for inspiration at home on the back deck*

About the Author

Frank J. Shima grew up in rural Southern Minnesota. After high school, he attended and graduated from the University of Minnesota.

He was the winner of the 1987 Lake Superior Contemporary Writers Series for fictional prose.

He has been a member of Tornado Alley Writers' Group since 1983. He was the screenwriter for *Doing Time*, an original half-hour comedy produced by the Screenwriters' Workshop, and wrote and produced *Junkyard Dog*, an original half-hour comedy in 1994.

His first novel *Vencil*, published in 2005, is also available from Beaver's Pond Press.

Visit the author's website at www.novelgems.com.

Acknowledgements

Special thanks to Dave and Michelle Stermer, Robin Juelich Shima, the Tornado Alley Writers' Group, and everyone else who gave of their time to assist me with this book.

Prologue

The car, with its lights off, slowed and turned onto a narrow gravel driveway that led to a secluded farmhouse, and then parked, concealed among a grove of trees just off the main county road. Three dark figures got out of the car and quietly closed the doors. Moonlight reflected off their shotguns as they started down the long driveway toward the farmhouse.

The sudden barking of two dogs broke the calm, night air.

Inside the house, eighty-year-old Nick Novacek put out his pipe and got up from his rocking chair.

"Hey Ted, Martin's finally here. And the supper dishes are still on the table."

His brother, Ted, started to clear the table but then stopped and turned to Nick.

"But I didn't hear his car."

"Strange. Neither did I."

Nick went to a living room window and pulled back the curtain. He strained to look out into the darkness.

"I don't see it out there, either."

Nick tensed as their dogs barked louder and more feverishly. Ted hurried from the kitchen to look out of another window. One of the dogs began to growl. Nick slowly moved from the window toward the front door.

"It's probably those damn raccoons back again."

A second later, a shotgun blast roared. A dog whimpered. "Nick! Quick, get the gun!" Ted shouted.

Nick turned and ran toward the gun rack in the far corner of the living room. Outside, another shotgun blast was

1

followed by a few moments of silence and then, footsteps pounding on the front porch.

Before Nick could reach his gun, the front door slammed open. Three hooded figures with guns stormed into the living room.

"Both of you! Up against that wall!"

Nick stopped and turned toward gunmen. He backed up slowly. Ted, looking confused and bewildered, shuffled over to stand next to his brother.

"What? What do you want?" Nick asked.

"The money. Just give us the money."

The two brothers looked at each other.

"What money?" Ted asked.

The intruder rushed in, grabbed Ted, and threw him to the floor against the far wall. He then held the barrel of the shotgun to Nick's throat.

"I said, give us the money!"

Chapter 1

A pickup truck approached and sped past me on the gravel road, leaving a giant dust trail in its wake. The driver, Jonas Flint, lifted one index finger from his grip atop the steering wheel. Just as it had been fifty years ago, it was still the standard wave in 1987 for farmers around the southern Minnesota town of Castle Rock.

As the dust settled, I spotted the two mailboxes at the end of Dale Paxton's driveway. One was a plain mailbox attached on top of a fencepost; the other, mounted upon a twelve-foot pole, was adorned with wings and the lettering "AIR MAIL."

I reached out of the right-hand window of the mail car and deposited the Paxton mail, mostly bills, into the lower box. Then, steering from what is usually the passenger side, I zigzagged on down the road toward Matt Ward's driveway. As I neared his mailbox, a miniature John Deere tractor, I looked down briefly to get his mail, and heard the sound of my car bang against the mailbox.

"Damn! Not again!"

The green and yellow of the tractor mailbox could be seen in the weeds, the post severed at the base. I got out and lifted the mailbox upright. It teetered for a few seconds and then fell in the other direction. After looking around to make sure no one had seen what had happened, I deposited the mail into the fallen mailbox and hurried off to my next stop.

Up ahead, I could see Mrs. Riley standing next to her mailbox, pretending not to be waiting for me. She reached behind her head and replaced an errant blonde curl. The wind picked up the hem of her pink flowered print dress, which she made no effort to keep down, showing a generous part of her beautiful long legs. I slowed to a stop next to her, being careful not to knock *her* to the ground with the mail car. I would have a tough time explaining that one to my boss, Ike. She leaned into the window to accept her mail.

"Care to come in for coffee, Martin?" she asked as her tongue seductively moistened her upper lip.

I had learned the first day that her idea of "coffee" was a lot different than mine. And, while nothing had happened that day or any other day, people in Castle Rock were convinced we were fooling around. That included her husband. One day I saw him standing at the mailbox waiting for me. At first I had been tempted to drive on by. When I did stop, he also leaned into the car window, but without seductively licking his lips. He did tell me what would happen to me if he ever caught me having "coffee" with his wife.

"Would you like to come in for coffee?" she asked again.

"No, thanks," I politely answered and carefully drove off. She would probably be waiting here for me tomorrow, and the next day, and the next. I knew if we fooled around just once, it would put an end to this. Even if Mr. Riley didn't catch us and he didn't do to me what he does to some of his bulls, Mrs. Riley would end up wondering why she ever waited for me at all. I knew I would only be a diversion in her life.

I glanced down at the seat next to me. I still had about six and a half feet of letters to deliver. At a hundred letters per foot, that was about 650 letters. To over a hundred more farms. I had already touched each piece of mail twice this morning. First, I had sorted the mail into bins, one for each farm. Then, I had loaded the contents of the bins into trays, starting with my last stop first. It seemed like everything was backward in this job.

I knew what to expect at the end of my route. Ike, my supervisor at the Post Office, would probably already have heard about the mailbox incident. He would threaten to write me up again. Then he would give me another "final" warning. If it weren't for me, he wouldn't have anything to do. Getting to the office and occupying space in an office was all that could be expected of him. Any interruption in this strenuous routine was not included in his job description.

When I reached the Novacek farm, it hit me. I had forgotten to stop by the previous night. The first Wednesday of every month was our night to play cards. It had completely slipped my mind. Since I was behind in my route, I decided to drive by after work to apologize.

I deposited the July issue of the *Farmer Magazine*, their milk check from the Credit River Creamery, and an oversized brown envelope into the mailbox, which stood at the end of a long, graveled driveway. The Novaceks' well-kept, one hundred-year-old house stood silently among some tall pines and cottonwoods. That was strange, since there always seemed to be more activity at their farm than any other. Usually when I stopped by with the mail, I would see horses at work on the fields. The Novaceks resisted change and used no tractors or heavy machinery. Now there was no sign of Nick or Ted.

Before I continued on my route, I took a final glance toward the farm. I noticed their cows were gathered outside the barn door. The Holsteins seemed anxious, constantly jockeying for position in front of the unopened barn door.

Nick and Ted hadn't milked these cows yet and the cows knew it. It wasn't like the Novaceks to neglect their chores.

I decided to go back and attempted to turn the mail car around on the narrow gravel road. The right front tire skidded over the gravel road. The car slid over the shoulder of the road and came to a stop with its nose at the bottom of the ditch and its rear end sticking in the air over the roadway.

"Damn! Not again!"

I still hadn't mastered driving from the wrong side of the car. I left the car in its awkward position, half on the road and half off, and headed on foot toward the Novacek farmhouse.

As I walked carefully across the cornfield, I avoided the tiny new stalks of corn, knowing that in a few months they would tower over me, bearing ears of corn ready for harvest. The Novaceks had recently cultivated their crop. The dirt between each row of corn was free of any weeds. Looking ahead at the calm farmstead, I wondered if I was doing the right thing. It wouldn't be the first time I had stuck my nose in where it didn't belong.

There was the incident with Mrs. Solak when I had heard muffled screams from the end of her short driveway. I had jumped from my car, had broken down the front door, and had brandished a kitchen knife on my way to the bedroom, the source of the commotion, only to find Charles Peterson. Mr. Peterson was an insurance salesman and a church elder but it didn't look like he was trying to sell her insurance or convert her to his religion. If he was, he had an interesting way of doing it. Before my awkward exit, I promised to keep my mouth shut for the sake of Mrs. Peterson, Fidelity Life Insurance, and Trinity Lutheran Church.

People thought I was too much of a snoop, but it wasn't easy to deliver mail in the small town of Castle Rock and the surrounding countryside without hearing gossip. Gossip was forced upon me at almost every mailbox. As much as I had tried, I hadn't mastered the art of driving with my fingers stuck in my ears.

The pungent odor of the barnyard mingling with the fragrance of roses greeted me as I approached the farmhouse. When I reached the Novaceks' front door, I listened for signs of activity inside the house and heard nothing. I tried to enter the front door but it was locked. That, in itself, was strange. The Novaceks never locked their doors. No one around here did. There was no crime in Castle Rock and no reason to lock one's doors. Also, it seemed as if they were always around, except for one night a month when they played bingo at the VFW.

I decided to mind my own business for a change and started back to get my car out of the ditch. The loud commotion from the cows outside the barn reminded me again that Nick and Ted were not farmers who left their cows unattended. Even if they had to leave on an emergency of some kind, they would have seen to it that someone would take care of their livestock.

"Nick! Ted!" I megaphoned my hands around my mouth and yelled toward the house. "It's Martin. Martin Prescott. I got your milk check here!"

Something was wrong if that didn't bring them out. Nick and Ted usually met me at the mailbox if they even suspected their milk money would arrive. Now, not even the dogs barked. They should have barked when I first set foot on their territory. They were well trained and knew the boundaries of the Novacek farm. I wandered out back toward the doghouse.

As I turned the corner, I found one of the Novaceks' dogs slumped against the side of the house, a bullet through his head and his blood splattered against the white paint. Fur inside the doghouse let me know the other dog was in there. It too was dead.

My next course of action should have been obvious. That was to walk across the road to Barton's farm to call Sheriff Trout. I, however, chose to investigate.

I attempted to force the front door open with a couple of hard shoves. Since I was only five foot ten and less than one hundred-fifty pounds, the solid oak door stood firmly in place while my shoulder reminded me why I carried mail instead of one hundred-pound sacks of feed. I decided against taking an ax to the door, mainly because I couldn't find one.

I went around to the rear of the house to check the back door. The rusty screen door to the back porch had been left wide open, but the door to the kitchen was locked. I peered in through the small window at the top of the door, cupping my hands around my eyes so that I could see into the darkness. Other than dirty dishes on the table, everything seemed to be in order. I moved around the exterior of the house trying to find another means of entry. I finally came to a tiny window that was open about a half an inch, and was able to pry it open, but only to the width of my head. I figured if my head would fit through, the rest of me would also. I scraped my way through the tiny opening, peeling my pants from my buttocks. I landed at the side of a bed, face-to-face with a filled spittoon. The pungent, sickening smell filled my nostrils before I was able to turn away.

"Hello, Nick. Ted," I shouted as I quickly stood up and pulled up my pants. There was no answer. I went out the bedroom door toward the kitchen. The old wood stove still gave off heat. I lifted the heavy, iron lid and saw the cold, gray ash speckled with just a few tiny red embers. I glanced toward the kitchen table where the supper dishes had not been cleared. The ticking of a clock competed with the sound of my own heavy breathing as I slowly edged along.

When I turned the corner past the stairway, I saw Ted sitting on the floor, propped up against the far wall. He was holding a shotgun that was pointed toward me.

I ducked back behind the staircase and then carefully peeked back into the living room, only to see that Ted was sitting in a giant pool of his own blood. As I carefully crept in to check on him, I accidentally kicked into a foot that lay in my path. It belonged to Nick, who rested in an almost identical position as Ted. His shotgun was pointed toward Ted. Both were dead, riddled with shotgun pellets.

Chapter 2

From his position in Nick's easy chair, Sheriff Trout thoroughly inspected the interior of the Novacek farmhouse. His three hundred-fifty pounds of mostly stomach and ass anchored him securely in place, just in case he might have the strange notion of getting up to look around. His real name was Trotcewski, which, when he was young, was shortened quite easily to Trots. Since being elected sheriff, some people decided the only respectful thing to do was refer to him as Trout. He shifted his old, wooden cane from one side of the chair to the other and used it to move a newspaper lying on the floor, as if he expected to find another corpse hidden underneath.

"Looks like suicide to me," Trout finally announced. One of his deputies stopped in the middle of lifting fingerprints while the other continued to outline Nick's body on the floor and the wall.

I could remain silent no longer.

"Suicide?"

"Well, one was a murder and the other was a suicide. Only thing left to figure out is which one did the murdering and which one did the suiciding."

"So now it's suicide and murder?" I asked.

"Or it could be they just killed each other," Trout answered.

"You can't be serious."

"Sure," Trout answered confidently. "It happens all the time."

"Not around here, it doesn't."

"It was bound to happen sooner or later. And who more likely than Nick and Ted here? Lord knows they had nothing left to live for. Trapped out here alone, together all these years," Trout said.

"It just doesn't make sense to me. I've known Nick and Ted for years, and if any two people knew how to get along, it was them."

"That's just what I'm getting at," Trout persisted. "Forty, fifty years of resentments all bottled up inside. Then, *kablooey!*"

I could see I was getting nowhere with that line of reasoning.

"What about the doors being locked? Don't you find that a bit strange?"

"Frankly, I would have been surprised if they hadn't been locked."

"How come we haven't found the key?"

I had tried to unlock the doors when I went to notify Trout of the Novaceks. I had been unable to find a key, which forced me to leave by the same bedroom window through which I had entered. And the deputies had not found the key in their search of the entire house.

"They probably hid it," Trout reasoned.

"Yeah, sure. They locked all the doors and hid the key before they blew each other away in fits of anger, after killing their two dogs first."

"It could happen," Trout argued.

Another of Trout's men, George, entered through the front doorway, avoiding the battered door which now hung loosely from a single hinge.

"I got someone to take care of the cows like you asked, Martin. And here's their mail here," he announced as he shuffled through the letters.

11

"Might as well have left it in the box," Trout snickered. "They won't be reading any of it."

I noticed there was something missing from the stack of mail that George handed to Trout.

"What happened to the large brown envelope, George?" I asked.

"Wasn't nothin' else out there," he said. "Else I woulda brought it in."

George appeared hurt that I might think he was incapable of doing a simple task like getting the mail.

"You sure there was an envelope to begin with, Martin?" Trout asked. "You deliver a lot of mail. Don't see how you can remember what you put in everyone's mailbox."

"Hell, I can remember what you got a week ago. Electric bill. Sears' catalog. The Castle Rock Sentinel. Plus a magazine that came in a plain brown wrapper. A magazine which I'm sure wasn't intended for Mrs. Trout."

Trout's face reddened as he shifted his weight as much as possible within the tight confines of Nick's chair.

"Don't you have something else to do besides interfering with an important police investigation?" he asked.

As I far I could see, they weren't doing anything to interfere with. However, I did have the rest of Grant Township waiting for their mail.

Chapter 3

With the help of Sheriff Trout's deputies, I got my car out of the ditch and continued with the rest of my morning route. Delivering the mail would help keep me from thinking about the scene at the farmhouse. Already guilt was creeping into the "raised Catholic" part of my mind. I was supposed to have been there the previous night. If I had been, perhaps I could have done something to prevent this from happening. Or maybe not. Maybe there would have been three dead bodies in the farmhouse now instead of two.

The smell of freshly cut alfalfa drifted in through the open windows. Most of the Novaceks' neighbors were out in their fields putting up their hay, something Ted and Nick had done a week earlier. That was just another reason I didn't agree with the sheriff's suicide theory. I couldn't see them going to all the trouble of baling hay first. I had helped a farmer bale one time and, if I had to do that again, I knew I'd sooner die first.

John Hartman's blue pickup appeared over the hill a mile down the road, a trail of dust spiraling behind him. My guess was that his baler must have broken down. Since he also was baling hay, it was about the only reason he would be headed for town. As I came to a stop at the end of Fat Tom Troba's driveway, Hartman passed me, giving me a wave. I waved at the back of the pickup as I shoved a *Wall Street Journal* into Fat Tom's mailbox. Missing a wave really irritated me. When I had first moved to Castle Rock five years ago after I turned thirty, waves from passing farmers were my first signs of acceptance. Most people didn't like me taking Art Siler's job. After all, Art was born and raised here and knew his way around the county with his eyes closed. The trouble was he handed out the mail the same way.

The Novaceks were the first to treat me as if I belonged. Everyone else wondered what a big shot from the cities was doing in their small town. At first, I wondered, too.

It was almost noon. Sarah would be waiting for me and I would be late. After the Novaceks, she had been the next to accept me in Castle Rock. She had become like a mother to me when I rented a room in her house after I moved to town. Even though I eventually moved out and bought my own place, Sarah still prepared lunch for me. She would probably already know why I was late. The rest of the morning route would have to wait.

Word of what had happened to the Novaceks would travel that fast. Sarah would be more upset than most about the Novaceks. She wasn't related to them but they were like family to her. Sarah's own parents had died suddenly when she was twenty-one. At that age, she'd been old enough to own a farm, but she had never been taught how to run one. It was the Novaceks who helped her through the first years until she could make it on her own.

It was a quarter past noon when I turned into her driveway. Sarah was standing on her porch with her hands on her plump hips. I tried to catch a glimpse of her face to determine her mood but she turned quickly on her heels and went into the house when she saw me.

The smell of freshly baked bread greeted me when I entered her kitchen. Sarah kept busy at the stove, her back to me as I took my spot at the table.

"It just doesn't make sense," she finally said with a voice barely above a whisper. A voice so tiny that it seemed it could not have come from such a huge body.

"That it doesn't," I agreed.

She turned and carried a bowl of soup from the stove, setting it on the table in front of me. I looked into her eyes, eyes that were struggling to hold back tears. Her lips quivered as she tried to keep everything in. Finally, she embraced me, my face to her bosom, as she started to cry.

"You're so good to me, Martin." She wiped her tears, and gave me a weak smile as she took the chair across from me. "Why couldn't I have had a son like you?"

"Probably the same reason I never had a mother like you," I answered.

Of course, it might have helped if she had gotten married. She did have her chances, though; in the thirty years since she had inherited the farm, she'd had more than her share of suitors. However, she always feared they were more interested in her farm than they were in her. Judging from the pictures of her from her younger years, she'd had nothing to worry about. Even now she still attracted widowers who obviously were after her for herself, not for the property. But now, she wouldn't settle for "seconds." These days it was probably more a fear of not being able to live up to a man's previous wife that kept her single.

"You could still get married," I reminded her.

"Naw. You came along thirty years too late," she joked as she turned away from me shyly. We ate the steaming hot chicken soup in silence for a few seconds before she looked up at me with a serious look on her face. "I always thought they'd live forever. Why do you figure they would just take their own lives like that?"

"I don't think they did."

"What do you mean?" she asked with a look of surprise on her face. "The sheriff told the reporters that it was a suicide."

"When have you ever known the sheriff to be right, about anything?"

"You think it was something else? That maybe someone killed them?"

"Too many things don't add up," I answered.

From the puzzled look on her face I guessed that she was trying to decide which was worse, the Novaceks killing themselves or somebody else brutally murdering them.

After lunch I knew I had to get back to my route but somehow sitting on the back porch with Sarah seemed more important, both for her sake and mine. In the hot summer sun, a slight breeze and shade made the porch even more desirable. I eased myself onto a cushioned rocker as Sarah stretched out on an old white porch swing that hung from two sturdy hooks anchored firmly to the ceiling. We sat in silence, a silence that made the calm of the countryside even more noticeable. It was one of those magical moments in the country when everything was at rest, causing me to feel that even time itself was resting. It was difficult for me to believe that, earlier, crime had intruded into these peaceful surroundings. When I had lived in Minneapolis, tragedy seemed more natural. There were no quiet moments in the city, where, for some, even a murder might be the most peaceful part of the day. It was a time when people would stop what they were doing long enough to notice what was happening around them.

"At least Nick and Ted won't have to slave in those hot fields again," Sarah finally said, as if that would be some consolation for dying. The trouble was that the Novaceks enjoyed working the fields.

"Yeah," I answered. "And they won't be sitting on any porches anymore either, not that they liked to do that much, anyway. Did you know of anyone who had something against them?" I asked.

"Enough to kill them? No. About the only thing they did that bothered people was that they drove too slow, backing up the traffic behind them."

People have been killed for less. Or just for being in the wrong place at the wrong time. But the Novaceks had been safe at home, supposedly. I felt that there was more to their deaths than just a random attack.

"They have any relatives?" I asked.

"Around here, no. There was a niece, though, who lives in Wisconsin. Nick said the last time they saw her she was only four years old, just after her mother died."

"That would be their sister?" I interrupted.

"Yes. Their only sister, Aggie. No other brothers. The little girl went to live with a grandmother in Milwaukee after Aggie's death. Her father had deserted them long before her mother's death."

"The little girl ever come back to visit?"

"No, and it's sad, too. Nick and Ted just adored that little girl. Of course, she wouldn't be a little girl any more. She'd be, let me see, twenty-five, maybe twenty-six years old now."

"How come Nick and Ted never got married?"

"Are you kidding?" she answered. "They hardly even looked at women. At least not the way *you* look at them. They just weren't interested. Not gay, but sort of non-sexual."

"I just figured they must have lost interest as they got older."

She paused and studied me closely as I got up to finish the route.

"Why all the questions?" she asked. "You going to do Trout's job for him?"

"Why not?" I answered. "Somebody has to."

Chapter 4

All the regulars at the Crow Bar had already heard about the death of the Novacek brothers by the time I had finished delivering the mail. Earl sat at the end of the long bar in his usual spot, where all the finish had worn down to the wood. Fifty of his seventy years had been spent at that bar. His stool with the yellow stuffing escaping from the torn red plastic was the nearest one to the men's room. A silhouette of a crow with a top hat marked that door, while the crow on the ladies' room wore high heels. However, strangers to the bar invariably made the mistake of entering the wrong one. It could have been avoided if the doors had been labeled properly, but that would have taken all the fun out of it.

Earl gulped down the last swallow of beer from his glass as he moved onto the stool next to mine.

"Too bad about the Novaceks, huh?" he asked.

What did he expect me to say? That it was good that they were blown away in their living room, rather than live out their miserable lives on that worthless piece of land they called a farm?

"Yeah, nobody deserves that," I answered, instead.

Earl waited patiently with his empty glass as Roy, the owner and only bartender of the Crow Bar, placed a glass of Grain Belt, Minnesota's finest, in front of me.

"Better get one for Earl here, too," I said.

A gleam appeared on Earl's face and his thick, red tongue licked his already moist lips while Roy refilled his glass.

Earl took a big swallow from his beer, a swallow that appeared to come straight from the bottom of his glass. He wiped a streak of white foam from his upper lip as he set down the glass.

"Yeah, it was too bad about the Novaceks," he repeated. He probably figured if it was enough to get one free beer, it just might work for another.

"Like I said, nobody deserves that," I said, thinking that maybe some people just might deserve it.

"I'm sure going to miss those guys," Earl said.

Earl spent all his days and nights in the bar so it seemed unlikely that he would really have been intimate friends with the Novaceks. He didn't have a car and I couldn't see him walking out to their farm.

"They used to have some Saturday nights here lately," he added.

The last I knew, the Novaceks always stayed home on Saturday nights. It was their night to stay up late an extra hour, until nine o'clock.

"When did they start coming in on Saturday nights?"

"Since about a month ago. Played cards with the Doherty brothers from Little Chicago, 'til they would all leave together at midnight."

I still couldn't picture the Novaceks out until midnight.

"You sure it was the Novaceks?"

"I figure I ought to know Nick and Ted when I see them. They were always good for two or three free drinks a night, apiece."

The Novaceks were never known for their generosity. If they had an extra cent, they were more likely to pinch it into two so they would have twice as much.

The Little Chicago boys I didn't know. They were from a different mail route. Zip code 55512.

The door to the bar opened and Sheriff Trout entered leaning on two over-burdened deputies, one under each arm. He was able to move about on his own, but not as quickly. Right now he was in a hurry to get to the bar. I wondered if his deputies were always that short or had shrunk over time from the weight of Sheriff Trout on their shoulders. They helped him onto the two stools next to mine, one for each cheek. Almost at the same time, Earl disappeared from his stool on my other side. Earl and Trout got along great together as long as they were in opposite sides of the same room.

Roy brought over a pitcher of Grain Belt, placed it in front of the sheriff, and waited for some money.

"This one's on the house, right?" Trout laughed as he lifted the pitcher to his lips with his pudgy hand.

"Yeah sure," Roy answered as he shrugged and ambled off to join Earl at the other end of the bar. Before he got there, Sheriff Trout had gulped down the last swallow, leaving the deputies with empty glasses in their hands. A beer just wasn't safe around Trout or Earl. That was probably one of the reasons they probably never sat together.

"Martin here doesn't think it could have been suicide," Trout announced loudly to the patrons of the bar. "Even after he found them with their own shotguns pointed at each other. No, I'm sorry to say it but the Novaceks killed themselves."

The regulars at the bar edged me away from Sheriff Trout and gathered close around him. Trout pulled a cheap cigar from his shirt pocket and bit off the end. He spit the end on the floor and turned toward a deputy who already had lit a match for him.

"Some people just can't accept the facts. They have to make things more complicated than they are."

Which meant that he wanted to do as little as possible? It should really have made no difference to Trout. He was at his best when he let his deputies do his work for him. It probably came down to the fact that the election was only months away and it wouldn't look good for him to have an unsolved murder on his record.

"How's the investigation going?" I yelled over the noise of the crowd gathered around Trout. "You are looking for the killers, aren't you?"

The bar crowd suddenly went silent as Sheriff Trout turned and glared at me.

"Hell, what's to investigate about a suicide, Martin? Any more stupid questions?"

There was plenty to investigate if Nick and Ted had been murdered, as I thought they had.

I decided not to ask any more stupid questions and moved over toward Earl, who was sneaking from table to table finishing off beers that had been left unattended and replacing each full glass he took with an empty one he had just finished. Roy watched, making no attempt to stop him. The customers would just have to buy more beer, which is what Roy wanted anyway.

"They'd just go flat, you know," Earl said through tobacco-stained, rotting teeth. "And I'd end up drinkin' them anyway. Most of the time, people don't even notice."

I wondered how many times I had drunk from a glass last touched by Earl's lips. It was enough to make a man quit drinking, at least around Earl anyway. I would just have to remember to hang on to my glass at all times.

"Anyone else besides the Little Chicago boys play cards with the Novaceks?" I asked.

"Not counting me, 'most everyone," Earl answered. "One time or another. Even Bud Helmsley over there. Didn't matter he lost all the time."

Bud, bald-headed with a paunchy stomach, listened intently as the sheriff continued with his sermon at the bar. Bud had just retired from the feed mill a couple of months ago and received three checks in the mail at the end of each month: social security, veteran's pension, and retirement. His wife had died a couple of years ago, leaving him alone in his house, a house in which he had raised seven children. He owned the house free and clear, which I knew since he no longer received mail with mortgage payment books from the bank.

"Can't understand how he could throw his money away like that," Earl grumbled as he followed me toward the bar, having finished the last of the abandoned drinks.

I figured Bud had plenty of money and he could do whatever he wanted with it, including lose it to the Little Chicago boys and the Novaceks if he wanted to. So what if millions of kids in the United States were starving to death and entire families wandering the streets homeless, and thousands of Earls had empty glasses in their hands.

"A guy works hard for his money. Don't see how you can part with it and not get something for it," Earl continued.

I didn't know what Earl knew about it, since he never worked and never had any money. Buying beer and drinks was okay but gambling was something Earl couldn't understand.

"Maybe they were just having a little fun with their money. You know what they say. You can't take it with you."

"Ah, bullshit," Earl said. "What could be fun about being cheated at cards?"

"You think the Little Chicago boys were cheating?"

"Well, they were winning. And in gambling, it's the only way a guy can win."

"Did you see them cheating?"

"No, but I wasn't exactly looking for it. I got better things to do."

"Refill?" Roy asked as he reached in front of me.

I checked the beer which I had left unguarded. Of course, it was now empty. And Earl's glass wasn't.

"No thanks, Roy," I answered. "I've had enough."

I noticed Sheriff Trout heading out the door and his fans were weaving back to their tables. I corralled Bud as he tried to move past me.

"Buy you a drink, Bud?"

Bud looked at his empty glass.

"Might as well," he answered, taking the stool next to me as Roy refilled the glass and placed it in front of him. "What's the occasion, Martin? Only time you ever buy is when you want to make a woman believe you're something you're not."

"Maybe it's the only time you ever notice," I replied.

"Well, I'm noticing now. What's it going to cost me?"

"Just answer me a few questions."

"I was afraid of that," Bud said, shaking his head from side to side. "Trouble is anything I tell you, the whole town's going to know before the sun goes down."

"Is there something you don't want the town to find out about?"

"Not to start out with," he answered as he squirmed on his stool. "But by the time it gets back to me, it will turn out that way."

I granted that he was right on that point and promised that anything discussed would be just be between the two of us. Surprisingly, Bud agreed.

"You figure the Little Chicago boys were cheating you?" I asked, deciding to get right to the point before Bud changed his mind.

"No way," he answered emphatically. "I wouldn't play in a game where I was being cheated."

"Earl here says they were always winning. Figures they must have been cheating."

"How the hell would Earl know? He don't know Q-tips from Kotex," he huffed. "No one was cheating anybody!"

"Were they that good or were you just that bad?"

"Just unlucky I guess," he answered.

"So, where did you and the Novaceks go with the Little Chicago boys after you left here every Saturday night?"

"That," he answered, "is none of your damn business."

That was it for the questions, because Bud left his beer and headed out the door, without even a goodbye. I followed him out, only to be greeted by Sheriff Trout, who was leaning against the squad car, his arms folded over his paunchy stomach.

"Just the guy I wanted to see," he announced as his deputies ushered me into the back of the sheriff's car.

Chapter 5

I sat alone in Sheriff Trout's squad car as the deputies tried to disperse the crowd that was gathering outside the bar. You would think they had never seen someone getting arrested before. Not that I was going to be arrested. At least I didn't think so. With Sheriff Trout, I couldn't be too sure.

As soon as the people were cleared from one side of the car, they would just move around to the other. It would have been easier to just drive away from the onlookers. Judging from the look on the sheriff's face, he seemed to be enjoying all the commotion. Finally, all that gawking must have made everyone thirsty and most of the crowd moved off the street and back into the Crow Bar.

Sheriff Trout opened the passenger door of the patrol car and squeezed through the door like a size ten foot into a size six shoe. The car took on a sharp lean to the right so that I was sitting more on the door than the seat. Sheriff Trout sat silently and fiddled with some papers.

"So you arresting me?"

"Hardly. There isn't anything I can arrest you for. Though nothing would make me happier than to throw you in our friendly jail."

Then do nothing, I was tempted to advise him but instead asked, "So what am I doing in here?"

"Nothing."

There was that word again. A perfect word for him and he used it well.

"Which is what I want you to do from now on," he continued. "You've been asking way too many questions."

"There's no law against asking questions, is there?"

Sheriff Trout turned his head toward the back seat slowly, which was the only way he could do it. I was surprised he could do it at all. Anger showed in Trout's eyes as he scowled at me.

"Listen, Prescott. I never cared much for you when you first came to town and would have preferred you'd never shown up here at all. But as long as you're living here, you're going to have to play by my rules."

"And just what are your rules?"

"Number one. I do the sheriffing. Number two. You don't."

Well, that sounded simple to me. But even if I would be willing to do my part, I had doubts about Trout holding up his end.

Finally Trout's face cleared and a poor imitation of a smile appeared. He looked like an exasperated parent trying to appease a stubborn child.

"Martin. I know you cared a lot for those brothers. Well, I did, too. Don't think I didn't. Sure I'd like to think things were different and that those boys didn't kill themselves. But sometimes you got to face facts and get on with it. Nothing you can do to help them now."

No, Sheriff, I thought. Nothing *you* can do.

Chapter 6

After driving around the county for an hour, Sheriff Trout was nice enough to drop me off at my house, about a mile outside town. That would have been okay, except that my car was still parked outside the Crow Bar. In a way, I appreciated Sheriff Trout's attempt at humor. I was just glad to be home and not locked up in the county jail, which Trout also would have considered humorous. I would just get a ride into town with the milk truck in the morning.

When I first moved to town, I wasn't sure how long I would stay. At first, renting seemed like the smartest way to go. When this old farmhouse went up for sale, it seemed like a good investment. After living in a cramped, noisy apartment building in the Cities, I welcomed the privacy of a farm home, surrounded by acres of corn, wheat, alfalfa, and pasture. I hadn't purchased any of the land. This prevented me from doing something crazy—like actually farming.

Darkness had already set in as I started down the quarter-mile driveway from the county road. Crickets and frogs alternately broke the silence as fireflies occasionally blinked on and off in the ditch along the road. Up ahead, the house itself was dark, shrouded by cottonwood and evergreen trees.

As I heard my own footsteps on the rutted gravel road, I got the strange feeling that I was not alone. Abruptly, I turned around to check if someone was following me. It was odd because it was the first time I had gotten that feeling out here in the country. Usually, it seemed like the rest of the world had deserted me.

The events of the day were getting to me. Afraid of one's own shadow. How many times had I heard that phrase and laughed? For one brief moment just now, I had been. However, the feeling that I wasn't alone didn't go away. If anything, it seemed to get worse.

I was relieved when I reached the front walk and the safety of my house. Just as I lifted my foot for the first step up to the porch, the screen door suddenly swung open. I heard heavy footsteps as a large figure moved about in the darkness of the front porch. The unmistakable form of a shotgun protruded into the night, barrel glinting in the moonlight and pointing directly at me.

"Hold it right there!" a deep voice called out.

I wasn't going anywhere. I wanted to fall to the ground in a heap but instead held my position rigidly with my right foot in midair.

"I figured you might be back," the voice continued.

Of course I would. I lived here didn't I?

I was blinded by a flash of light that I first thought was from the blast of the shotgun. I imagined myself suffering the same fate as Nick and Ted. Instead, my eyes made out a man's shape silhouetted against the porch light.

"Why it's you, Martin," the voice exclaimed. The barrel of the shotgun was no longer pointed between my eyes. "What you doing walking home? Where's your car?"

"Sheriff gave me a ride home."

My eyes cleared enough to make out that the figure was Ed Bartlet, the neighbor who used to own the house. He still owned and farmed the land as well as the adjacent one hundred sixty acres he had bought from his grandfather.

"What's the big idea, Ed?"

Ed sheepishly ushered me into the house, as sheepishly as a man six-foot-six and two hundred seventy-five pounds can look anyway.

"I heard the commotion here earlier when I was out on the field. Thought I should check it out."

"Check what out?"

Ed just turned on a light and pointed toward my living room. It had been totally ransacked. Paintings I had collected had been smashed and ripped. My stereo equipment would play music no more. Papers were scattered and furniture overturned and cut, stuffing laying about the floor. My bust of Mark Twain was stuffed through the picture tube of the television set.

"Rest of the house looks okay," Ed said as he moved a ruddy hand through his tousled hair. His kind, blue eyes tried to comfort me through the confused look on his face. "Why just this room? Can't understand it. Unless they must have found what they were looking for."

"Must have," I answered.

Was it just a coincidence that I had been detained in the squad car while my living room was being torn apart? Or had I been kept occupied until someone—maybe even some of the deputies—had finished destroying my home. It would even explain the mysterious ride home. Sheriff Trout probably drove me around the county until he was sure they were finished.

"I'll call the sheriff for you if you want," Ed finally said.

"No, he's probably got better things to do."

"At least let me help you clean up," Ed offered.

I could see he was sincere. It probably bothered him as much as it did me that his childhood home looked as it did.

"No, that's okay Ed. I figure I'll just leave it this way for a while."

That really confused Ed.

"Whatever you want. It's your place, so I guess you keep it any way you want it."

He shrugged his shoulders, picked up his shotgun and headed out the door.

I looked over the room and sat on one of the two lumps of stuffing which had once been my favorite chair. In a way, I sort of liked the way things looked, like my apartment during my last two years of college.

Chapter 7

The next morning, I woke up to the sharp glare of sunlight piercing its way into the living room through torn curtains. It was a rude introduction to another day, a sudden reminder to me that things were not normal. My "Poseidon Adventure" living room only reinforced that fact. The appearance of the room had not improved over the night, which disproved the theory that things were supposed to look better in the morning. I stood up slowly, the kink in my back preventing me from doing otherwise, and moved into the kitchen to start some coffee.

I looked up at the face of the large, green teapot clock above the sink. It was only five o'clock, earlier than I had thought. Time was moving along slowly. The previous day had seemed like it lasted an eternity, as had the other periodic painful days of my life, while the happiest days of my life passed by quickly. Perhaps if I had led a more painful life I would be a lot younger now, but wishing I was older.

Peter pulled his long, white milk truck into the yard, earlier than usual. I threw some clothes on and ran outside. It didn't give me time to shower; I would do that at my old room at Sarah's during lunch, as I had done many other days. Peter didn't appear too surprised to find me waiting as he hoisted his muscular body back up into the cab.

"Saw your car in town this morning," Peter said in a low, gravely voice that slowly crawled out of his heavily bearded face. "And when I saw the lights on in your place, I figured you might be needing a ride."

"Nothing gets by you, does it, Peter?"

"Not as long as I notice."

"The Novaceks ever talk to you about the Crow Bar on Saturday nights?"

Peter thought that one over for a while as he shifted the tanker into first gear and started out the long driveway.

"All they ever talked to me about was their milk. And how it was better before I got the tanker and hauled their milk in cans. They never did forgive me for getting this new truck."

"And they never mentioned anything about the boys from Little Chicago?" I asked.

Peter chuckled as he maneuvered his truck down the center of the gravel road that led to town. "There's lots of boys from Little Chicago. But, as far as I know, Nick and Ted didn't know anyone from there."

"Did you ever see anyone suspicious hanging around their farm? Any strangers?"

"You mean besides you?" he answered, half humorously and half seriously.

I had that coming. After all, I was still a stranger in town. An outsider. It would take me more than five years to lose that label. Most of the people who were here before I arrived would probably have to die first.

"I heard Nick and Ted were into gambling lately."

Peter slowed his truck down to a stop at the four-way on the edge of town and turned to look into my eyes for a few seconds.

"Now, gambling. There's something we talked about. And the craps games we used to have outside their milk house at six in the morning."

"Craps?"

"Sure. And did you know they had a roulette table set up in their hayloft? Though you never could get a true roll when the loft was filled with bales. Always came up eleven but no one ever caught on. And the blackjack games! Why, they used to fly in dealers from Las Vegas just so the house, I mean, barn could have an edge."

I got out and walked the rest of the way to my car.

The parking ticket on my windshield was just another indication of Sheriff Trout's warped sense of humor. Somehow I was illegally parked on a snow emergency route although it was the middle of summer. An ordinary parking ticket was only three dollars but the snowbird ticket went for twenty-five. If Trout was trying to annoy me, he was doing a good job of it.

Chapter 8

The morning delivery went slowly. When I got to Sarah's house, I saw she was out in the fields. In the kitchen, I found a sandwich on the table, which she usually left for me if I was late and I was to eat alone. After finding a fresh towel in the linen closet, I went into my old room and closed the door behind me. As I disrobed for my shower, I glimpsed at myself in a mirror on the dresser. My once flat stomach had now taken on the paunch that I had always noticed in older men. I flattened my stomach with my hand and opened the door to the adjoining bathroom.

It was I who screamed, not she. And even though we were equally naked, it was I who went through the frantic ritual of trying to position my towel in the appropriate places. It hadn't occurred to me that all I had to do was close the door. After I had closed the door, I wondered why. She, whoever she was, had the most beautiful body that I'd ever had the pleasure of seeing naked.

I hurriedly pulled on my clothes, just as she came out of the bathroom wearing a robe. I didn't believe it possible, but she looked even sexier. Her light blue robe, which matched her sexy, blue eyes, clung to her waist and yet hung loosely over her breasts.

"You must be Martin Prescott," she said in a smooth voice that showed no hint of anger, embarrassment, or fear.

"Yes. And you are . . .?"

"Diane. Diane Crowley. Nick and Ted's niece from Milwaukee."

Not exactly as I had envisioned her. I stood silently, staring at her for a few seconds.

"If you were expecting Sarah, she's working outside right now."

"You mean . . .? No! No, it's not like that," I answered, trying to make the truth sound as convincing as possible. "I knew Sarah was outside."

I gathered up my shoes and socks and headed toward the kitchen.

"I'd better let you finish in there while I eat my lunch."

*   *   *

I waited anxiously for Diane. What was she doing in the bath that long? Maybe she was waiting for me to leave. Though she didn't seem too upset about what had happened. I wondered if I had made a bad first impression. My first impression of her would last forever.

It wasn't until after I was married that I first saw my ex-wife, Patty, naked. Even though she was pleasant to look at, I had to admit I was a little disappointed. For some reason, she seemed ashamed of her body. The only time I was allowed to view her naked was in bed in the moonlight. Full moons were a special treat for me. It always amazed me how she could throw off the covers, get out of bed, and put on a robe in one motion. If I saw any skin at all, it was the bottom of her feet as she hurried to the bathroom.

And it wasn't until after our first anniversary that I finally saw her fully naked under a bright light. Even then, it was by accident. I'd overslept one morning, which I usually never did. Thinking I was gone, Patty walked naked into the bedroom, looking so beautiful and innocent. Until she saw me. She accused me of lying in wait for her, making me feel so guilty and so ashamed that after that, I had a difficult time looking at her at all. Especially into her eyes. I could hardly remember her face any more but her feet were indelibly etched upon my brain.

That was why I was so surprised that Diane wasn't upset, not only at my seeing her but her seeing me. I didn't think Patty ever actually saw me naked. While making love, she always had her eyes firmly closed. If there was any chance that she might see anything of me other than my hands or face, she discreetly shielded her eyes with her hands. I was sure that another man could have spent a whole week in her bed without her realizing that it wasn't me. Which probably explains how it eventually happened.

The outside door opened and Sarah walked in from the field, sweat dripping from her forehead and soaking through under the armpits of her blue work shirt. She looked at me curiously.

"I'm surprised you're still here. Won't you be late for your afternoon route?"

"That's okay. Let them wait."

"Good. Then you can meet Diane, Nick and Ted's niece," she said. "I've told her so much about you. She's anxious to see you."

Chapter 9

It was Sarah's idea for Diane to accompany me on my route. Sarah would be busy with her chores, which would have left Diane alone in the farmhouse.

I looked over at Diane, her long blond hair flowing in the wind as she looked out at the countryside. She must have sensed me staring at her, for she suddenly turned quickly toward me. She smiled, looking more embarrassed now than when I had seen her earlier. With a puzzled look, she waved her arms in front of her.

"It doesn't seem right," she said. "Sitting here on this side with no steering wheel. Not driving."

"I know what you mean," I answered. "For the first few weeks, I thought I was driving in a mirror. Even had trouble telling right from left."

She looked out over the fields again as I stopped at Mrs. Henrikson's mailbox. There was no mail for her but the red flag was up which meant it contained mail to be sent out. At least it was supposed to. Her kids seemed to think it was funny to tamper with that flag, which rendered the flag useless. Sure enough the box was empty. For some reason, I turned the flag down again as I pulled away.

When Diane turned back to me, she seemed much more serious.

"Did you know them well? Uncle Nick and Uncle Ted?"

"About as good as anyone around here, except for Sarah, that is."

"I remember them from when I was a little girl. Uncle Ted always treated me like a princess. That's what he called me. Princess. Then he'd point out over the farm and say, 'All this will be yours some day.' This farm was their whole life."

She stopped briefly and closed her eyes and took a breath.

"I really should have come back to see them. But I wasn't sure if they'd even remember me." She stopped again, shaking her head. "That's not exactly true. I got busy with my own life and forgot about everything back here." She looked over to me, as if she wanted me to forgive her.

"That's it, isn't it!" she exclaimed as she sat erect in the seat and craned her neck to look farther across the farmland.

We had finished the afternoon half of the route and were headed back to town on the winding gravel roads. Out of habit, I had taken the shortest route back to town on the road that passed Nick and Ted's place.

"That's my uncles' place! I still remember it. Let's stop and look around," Diane continued.

I wondered if that would be a good idea. After all, it was a murder scene and I didn't want to disturb any evidence. Then again, if there was any evidence to be found, Trout certainly wouldn't find it. Besides, who had more right to be on the property than Nick and Ted's own niece?

I turned the car into the long, narrow driveway. It was strange, but in just this short time, Nick and Ted's place seemed to be falling into disrepair. The front door was boarded up with a piece of weathered plywood. The weeds were already starting to set in and were taking over the grass around the house. After I came to a stop in the farmyard near the silent windmill, Diane slowly opened her door and stuck one long leg out, causing her skirt to ride up for a moment. She stood outside the car and smoothed her short skirt down her thighs. She leaned her head back into the car.

"Let's go inside," she said in an almost devilish voice.

"Do you think that's such a good idea?" I asked. I hadn't counted on her wanting to go inside the house. "I really don't think we should be in there."

"Ah, you're just being scaranoid," she answered.

"Scaranoid?"

"Yes, scaranoid. I can thank my mom for that."

She started toward the house. It was clear she was going inside, no matter what I decided.

I joined her, and we slowly circled the house looking for a way of entry. This seemed all too familiar. Since the front door was boarded up, we checked all the windows as I had the day I found the Novaceks. Even the window I had used before was closed tight, which was a disappointment to me. I would have given anything to watch Diane crawl through that window. Finally, we reached the front door again.

"Short of forcing off the plywood," I said. "There's no way to get in."

"So, what are we waiting for?" she asked as she climbed onto the porch. She jammed her slender fingers between the plywood and the door and pulled with all her weight.

"Well, aren't you going to help?"

"Sure, but not like that."

I went to my car and got the tire iron from underneath the front seat. When I returned, Diane was still impatiently attempting to pull off the plywood. What was in there that she was so eager to see? As I pried the plywood from the door, she looked like a little girl unwrapping a Christmas present, her eyes wide open with excitement. I had bent the plywood open only about a foot when she stopped me and

40

squeezed through into the house as I held the four-inch nails from her clothes. It took me a few more minutes before I was able to fully remove the plywood and follow her inside. I decided to leave the plywood up in case Trout or one of his men happened by.

Diane was nowhere to be seen. It might have been my imagination but the air still smelled of shotgun powder as I entered the dark living room. I could make out the white outlines of Nick and Ted on the floor and walls. I called out to Diane but there was no answer. I listened for her, but all I could hear was the ticking of the clock on the mantel. This Diane was a strange one. I had expected her to react differently. After all, she was in the house where her uncles were violently murdered. She showed no apprehension or fear. Rather, she seemed to thrive in the excitement of it. What was she doing now? Looking for clues? Or concealing evidence?

Finally, the floor squeaked above me. I hurried up the stairs and found her in a storage room. An old desk, its top worn from fifty years of arms and elbows, sat in front of a small window that faced out over the barn. Old shoes and winter boots were lined up beneath heavy coats that hung on sturdy, ornate hooks on the wall. Butter churns, wash tubs, kerosene lanterns and other items that might soon bring a good price at an auction added to the clutter in the small room. The ceiling angled sharply from the floor until it reached its highest point of six feet at the opposite wall. I crouched my way toward her as she sifted through an old cardboard box.

"I found it!" she finally exclaimed. I expected her to be holding a pile of money or jewels. Instead she held a stack of old photographs. "My mom destroyed all the old pictures when my dad left."

As she shuffled through the photographs, she stopped when she came to an old wedding picture.

"This is my mom and dad. I haven't seen my dad for twenty years. My mom always told me what an evil man he was and how mean he was to me. But I can't remember any of that. You know, he used to tell me a story each night and then sing me to sleep. I wonder what he looks like now."

"See, here are Uncle Nick and Ted," she said as she pointed them out. "I thought maybe I would have forgotten what they looked like or changed them to other people."

She wiped the dust off Nick and Ted's picture and slowly looked up. "Sarah said that you don't think my uncles killed themselves."

"That's right."

"Your sheriff thinks otherwise. He told me that all the evidence points to a suicide."

"Well, that's just the problem. I don't think Trout would know evidence if it jumped up and bit him on the ass."

"It sure is a big enough target," she said. I was glad to see the smile come back to her face.

Chapter 10

Diane and I walked through the woods on paths worn down from generation after generation of cows on their journeys between the barn and the pasture. Her long muscular legs threatened to propel her far ahead of me as I struggled to keep up.

"I don't think my uncles killed themselves either," Diane finally said, as she stopped to look out over the pasture. "Look. They had so much to live for. All this beautiful land. My mom said it was their whole life. That they'd rather die than lose it."

She turned to look at me.

"That's probably what happened, isn't it?" It was more of statement than a question.

Before I could say anything she suddenly removed her shoes and broke into a run, her skirt flying up and exposing more of her deeply tanned legs. I turned back for a moment to see if someone might be following us. When I turned around again, it was just in time to see her disappear up the path, over a rise in the woods.

As much as I despised running, I decided to give it a try anyway, although it was more of a jog or a home run trot. The last time I had really run was during my last few months in the Twin Cities. But then, I was running for my life. Who would have thought a thirty-year-old, recently divorced mailman could get into so much trouble?

Back then, I blamed the whole world for my failed marriage and made sure the whole world knew it. I took advantage of each rare opportunity to sleep with women I met in bars. That was, until a man who strongly resembled Brutus of Popeye fame caught me in bed with his Olive Oyl.

It was when the angry husband chased me down a dark alley with a butcher knife in his hand and me, in just my jockey shorts, that I decided I needed a change in my lifestyle. Therefore, the move to Castle Rock. Castle Rock, where everyone seems to know everything about everyone else and each woman is someone's wife or not-to-be-violated daughter.

When I finally caught up with Diane, she was sunning herself in a secluded spot beside a stream that flowed through the pasture. She wore a two-piece swimsuit which I could only assume she had worn underneath her clothes. Her blouse and skirt lay in a pile next to her. Beads of water glistened off her skin as her hair hung in wet strands down her back.

"You look like you could use a swim," she said.

"I would except I wasn't as prepared as you."

"Don't let that stop you," she laughed.

I slowly stripped off my shirt and sat down to remove my shoes and socks. When I stood up to unbuckle my belt, I noticed that her eyes were riveted on me. What made me think that she would discreetly turn her head as I disrobed? I casually pulled down my pants, leaving me in just my underwear. This was the moment of truth. There was no reason to be embarrassed about completely disrobing in front of a woman, even one I hardly knew, especially when she'd already gotten a glimpse of me. I had done it many times.

But it seemed different when it was after a night of drinking and before jumping into bed. It was almost unexciting. I felt I would be exposing my inner soul to Diane if I pulled my shorts down past my ankles. I couldn't do it. I wondered if this was how my ex-wife had felt about undressing in front of me.

As I slid into the cool water of the stream with its sandy bottom, I noticed that Diane was no longer looking at me but staring up at the clouds. As uncomfortable as I had been a few seconds earlier, I was now hurt that she now seemed disinterested. I could have been naked and she wouldn't have noticed. After floating in the stream for a few minutes, I got out and joined her in the sun to dry off.

"I think we should do it," Diane finally announced through closed eyes.

"What?"

"I think we should find out who killed my uncles."

Chapter 11

After I dropped Diane at Sarah's, I headed to the post office to leave off the outgoing mail. It was nearly six o'clock, almost three hours later than usual. I hadn't counted on a partner in my attempt to find the real killers of the Novaceks. This made it seem more official. Before, I could just have given up if I had wanted to. Now, I would have to answer to Diane. I wasn't sure that was something I wanted to do. Her last words to me at Sarah's were instructions. Find out about the Doherty brothers. Nothing was said about the day she had just spent with me. I had no idea whether she enjoyed it as much as I had.

At least I had found out something about her on our way to Sarah's. It explained why she was so independent. No, she wasn't married. Or even living with anyone. That was good. She had many friends who were men, as she put it. That didn't surprise me. She lived alone in Milwaukee, even owned her own house on Lake Michigan. Surprising for such a young woman. She had practically raised herself, again as she put it, and graduated with honors from high school and Marquette University. Now she was a top executive at a leading advertising firm in Milwaukee. I also didn't feel so bad about not being able to keep up with her when she ran off in the pasture. She regularly ran marathons in less than four hours, confident she would be able to complete one in less than three hours within a few years.

Confidence. She exuded it. Just sitting next to her, walking with her and talking to her, I could feel it. It made me even more confident in myself. I had no doubt that, between the two of us, we could do anything. Even do Trout's job for him.

I got to the post office in time for the outgoing mail to be sorted and sent out to their proper destinations. I was called into Ike's office as soon as I entered the door.

"About time you saw fit to make it back in here," Ike grunted as he eyed me from my supervisor's office. Ike was the perfect matching bookend to Sheriff Trout. They weren't related but hung around together as they grew up. From behind, you couldn't tell them apart. Not only did they look alike, they did about the same amount of work.

"And don't give me any story about a flat tire," he continued. "Unless it includes something about that pretty young girl from Milwaukee."

Rather than answer, I just turned to leave. I'd found out long ago that the best way to get along with Ike was to ignore him.

"Before you go," Ike yelled after me. "You're getting a little sloppy with your work. This here envelope for the Novaceks turned up at Joe Tuma's place."

He tossed the envelope on the desk in front of me. It looked exactly like the one I had deposited in the Novacek mailbox. Right down to the date on the postmark. Except I knew it couldn't have been the same one. This envelope lay perfectly flat on Ike's desk while I had to fold and crease the original to fit it into the mailbox.

Chapter 12

The sun was setting directly over the road ahead as I peered under the visor. For some reason, all traffic seemed to be headed toward me from the opposite direction. I felt like I might be missing something in Castle Rock. Either that or they had to evacuate Little Chicago and I was headed directly into some natural disaster. Of course, meeting up with the Doherty brothers could be a disaster in itself.

I tried to convince myself that it was my own idea to drive to Little Chicago, not Diane's. After all, I had planned to go there on Saturday night when there would be a better chance to find them in town. Going there now would give me a chance to nose around town without pressure and find out where they would hang out.

When I reached the town limits, I discovered I wouldn't have to do too much nosing around. The whole town was hardly larger than a city block or two, counting St. Scholastica, whose steeple stood high above the rest of the town. The front steps of the Catholic Church seemed to spill directly into the front door of Dillinger's, the only bar in the town. Judging from the cars and pickup trucks parked outside, Dillinger's definitely was the place to be. The rest of the town consisted of a combination grocery store and gas station, a feed mill, and a few houses.

I parked my car as close to Dillinger's as I could, near the edge of town, and walked slowly toward the front door. Even from a half-block away, I could hear the loud, country music and noise of the crowd gathered inside. When I reached the dirt- and beer-stained front door, it slammed open into my extended right hand. A heavy-set farmer in work boots, overalls, plaid shirt, and green co-op cap breathed a beer-scented "watch it, buddy" at me as he brushed past. At least there would be room inside for me now. Or so I thought. As I tried to enter the crowded, smoke-filled bar, I was continually shoved back toward the door. I found it difficult to believe that the heavy-set farmer had left voluntarily. Three people probably came in the back door, which caused Dillinger's to spit the farmer out the front door.

I decided to ease my way in and go in whatever direction the crowd would take me. Go with the flow, so to speak. After a few minutes inside, I was only halfway to the bar but had moved across the room from the front door. Along the way, people shouted words to me which I couldn't hear and which I answered with just a nod or shake of my head.

A slightly attractive girl in her early twenties flashed a toothy smile and then embraced me, crushing her generous breasts against my chest. She whispered a breathy "Good to see you again, Chuck. Where you been keeping yourself?" into my ear and then planted a sloppy kiss on my lips. The demands of the crowd pulled us apart and carried her in another direction. I found myself wishing I was this lucky Chuck as I watched her disappear into the maze of swirling customers. I then came to an abrupt halt as I was forced into a mountain of man with his hands on his hips, stern look on his face and his eyes darting back and forth between me and the direction of the girl. Now I really wished I was Chuck. The stalemate lasted for about a half a minute until three high school boys in lettermen's jackets, three of the many who shouldn't have been in the bar, pushed me along with them in their haste to reach the bar.

This was turning out to be a complete waste of time. If the Doherty brothers were here, how would I find them? And what good would it do? For all I knew, the "mountain" could be one of them. He didn't strike me as one who would be willing to do much talking, especially to me.

I reached the bar and tried to get the attention of the bartender, a slightly smaller version of the mountain I'd just encountered. In my loudest voice, I asked for a beer. The bartender returned with a glass of foam for which I was charged two dollars. At least it wouldn't take me long to finish my beer and leave.

There was a clink of my glass as I felt an arm at the small of my back, a slender, feminine arm. I turned expecting to be reunited with the girl. Instead, I stared into the toothless grin of a haggard, seventy-year-old barfly. She attempted to pull me closer towards her when the crowd fortunately separated us and moved me down the bar.

It turned out to be as big a chore to leave the bar as it had been to enter. When I was finally able to pry myself out the back door, I inhaled a deep breath of smoke free air. My legs felt unsteady and almost unable to bear my weight, as I'd been buoyed by the crowd for so long. I leaned back against the wall and stared up at the star-filled sky.

"So this where you disappeared to," called a female voice. I peered out into the darkness. The barfly made her way out of the shadows. "Least you coulda done is bought me a drink."

She sat on the lower step, pulled an unfiltered Camel from her purse, and lit it with a shaky hand.

"So what you doing in Dillinger's?" she asked. "I mean, besides not buying me a drink?"

"You know the Doherty brothers?" I asked.

"Sure. Who doesn't?"

"I don't."

"I guess you're the lucky one then." She had to laugh at that, a laugh that was accompanied by the exhale of cigarette smoke and then interrupted by a coughing fit.

"They inside?" I asked when she had quit coughing.

"No. If they was, you woulda known it. It wasn't a good idea for you to hit on Roxanne, like you did."

I thought back to my encounter with the girl in the bar.

"But she's the one who made the moves on me," I explained. "She just got me confused with someone else."

"Hell," she chuckled as she eyed me up and down. "You don't look any more like Chuck than I do. If I was you, I'd go someplace that wasn't here."

There wasn't any reason for me to stay around anyway. It was obvious I wouldn't find the Doherty brothers. From what I had just heard, it would probably be better if I didn't. I moved down the steps toward my car. When I reached the drunken lady, I pulled some money from my wallet and placed it in her wrinkled hands.

"Least I can do is buy you a drink."

She smiled up at me. With a wink, she got up and headed toward the back door of the bar. After she disappeared into the bar, I turned toward my car and came face to face with the mountain man and four slightly smaller mountains. They wore identical jackets with the lettering "LITTLE CHICAGO TRACTOR PULL." I could just see these guys out in some field, each pulling a tractor around. They formed a circle around me, standing with their hands on their hips, squinting their eyes, and sneering at me.

"I was just leaving, guys."

"Not yet you're not," the mountain growled. They each took a step closer to me, making me feel like I was being

51

swallowed up by a giant hand. "We don't care for strangers coming in here and hustling our women."

I was firmly grabbed from behind; my arms pulled back so hard it felt like they were being torn from their sockets. The mountain man moved toward me with the swiftness of a cat and brought his knee up into my groin. The pain shot up to my head and an overpowering blackness filled my brain. My knees buckled beneath me and I was thrown to the ground. A hard boot caught me under the ribs. I took the fetal position and prepared myself for more. The ground shook as they moved toward me again.

"Boys! Stop that!" a woman's voice cried out from what seemed like another world.

"But Ma," the mountain man answered.

"I said stop that. Just leave him alone."

One by one, the five men reluctantly moved away, but not before stomping me flat on the ground face first. I squinted up into the light to see the last of them disappear into the bar and the face of the barfly looking down at me.

She sat next to me on the ground and pulled a pint of whiskey from her purse.

"Here. Have some of this."

She lifted my head into her lap, and held the bottle to my lips like she was feeding milk to a baby. A couple of hard swallows helped me forget about the pain.

"It's a good thing you came out when you did. They could have killed me."

"Ah, they was just having some fun."

I rolled off her lap and got into up on my hands and knees.

"I'm glad your boys listen to you."

"They ain't my boys," she laughed. She took a drink from the whiskey bottle and lit another Camel.

"But they called you Ma," I said, managing to sit up onto my haunches. "And they obeyed you."

"Everybody calls me Ma. And the reason they listen to me is because they're afraid of my boys."

If they were afraid of her sons, I sure as hell didn't want to meet up with them. Then it finally came to me.

"Then you must be the Doherty boys' mother?"

"Yep. Ma Doherty."

*   *   *

We sat on the back steps passing the bottle back and forth. More and more people crowded into Dillinger's and the noise inside turned itself up another notch.

"So why are you looking for my boys," Ma Doherty asked.

I knew I had to phrase this correctly. I didn't want her to get the wrong idea. I didn't really want to leave without finding out something, especially after what I had just gone through.

"I just wanted to talk to them."

"Hell. What would my boys know that would interest you?"

"Two of my friends from Castle Rock were killed the other day."

"Oh, I heard about that," she said. "Except the way I heard it, one of them killed the other before doing himself in."

"I don't think that's the way it happened," I said.

She stiffened up, holding the bottle close to her.

"You think my boys had something to with it, don't you?"

"No," I answered quickly.

"Bullshit," she said as she got up quickly. "My boys may be a lot of things. But they wouldn't kill anyone. And if they did, they sure as hell wouldn't need a gun."

She walked up the steps and disappeared inside the bar.

Chapter 13

The long drive back to Castle Rock from Little Chicago gave me ample time to think things over. I had been so sure that the Doherty boys had killed Nick and Ted. While I couldn't discount them, I wondered if they even had a motive for the killings or even the opportunity. If they were anything like the yahoos I had encountered in Little Chicago, they probably didn't need a motive. And as Ma Doherty had told me, they didn't need a gun either.

Bud Helmsley was still a possibility. He played cards with the Novacek brothers on Saturday nights also. What reason would he have to kill Nick and Ted? They had been friends since childhood. As far as I knew, Bud wasn't hurting for money.

I also had to wonder what part Sheriff Trout had in all of this, if any. Though it could be that Trout wasn't covering anything up; maybe he was just totally inept. Since there hadn't been a murder in this county in the last forty years, he could hardly be expected to be an expert.

I hated to admit it, but the person with the most to gain from the death of the Novaceks was Diane. She was their only living heir and was sure to inherit all they had.

The rumor around town was that Nick and Ted had a million dollars saved up. Knowing how people exaggerate, it wouldn't surprise me if the Novaceks had nothing put away. However, the farm itself had to be worth a couple hundred thousand.

As far as I knew, Diane was in Milwaukee at the time of the murders, though I had only her word for it that she didn't need the money.

I checked my watch as I slowed for the turnoff to my house. I was surprised that it was only ten o'clock at night and not two or three in the morning. So I continued on past the turn and headed for Sarah's. There was a chance that Diane might still be up, and I wanted to relate my findings with her. It also seemed like an excellent excuse to see her again.

I stopped when I reached the end of Sarah's driveway. All of the lights inside the house were already off, with only the yard light illuminating the farmyard. If only there was some way of waking Diane without disturbing Sarah. She probably wouldn't appreciate being bothered in the middle of the night just so I could talk to Diane. As much as I wanted to see Diane, I decided it could wait until the morning. I turned the car around and was about to head back home when, miraculously, a light came on in the kitchen.

I backed the car down the driveway and parked it in the farmyard. Neither Sarah nor Diane poked a head out of the screen door to investigate. I slowly crept up the steps of the front porch. As I passed by the kitchen window, I stopped to peek inside. It wasn't Sarah's or Diane's shape that wandered about the kitchen. Instead, a large man about fifty years old rifled through cabinets and drawers obviously so intent on finding whatever he was looking for he had not heard me drive up. The man, red-faced and pot-bellied, wore an outdated green leisure suit that may have fit him at one time but now looked about three sizes too small. I stood and watched as the man continued his search. A chill crept up my back, causing me to shiver despite the late night air. I had already encountered one gruesome murder scene and it was surely enough to last me a lifetime. Where were Sarah and Diane? If this was the man who had killed the Novaceks, what was to stop him from doing the same to Sarah and Diane or to me?

I quietly searched around outside, looking for something that I could use to defend myself. The garden rake I came upon first looked like a possibility. Upon picking it up, I could tell it was too flimsy to deter the man in the kitchen. I discarded it and searched further until I came upon a double-bladed ax near the woodpile. This would do, I decided, as I headed back toward the kitchen. I wondered if I would even have to the nerve to use it. If this man had killed the Novaceks and maybe the women, yes, I felt I could. The man probably would have a gun. What good would an ax do against a gun? Then again, I figured, the thing I had on my side was the element of surprise.

I carefully looked inside the kitchen window again. The man was now standing at a counter with Diane's purse in his hands, searching through its contents. I thought for a second of going for help. But what good would Sheriff Trout do? And if Sarah and Diane weren't already dead, I didn't want to waste even the little time it would take to contact the sheriff.

I closely surveyed the kitchen. Off in the far corner I could see that the door from the basement was open. That was it. I sneaked over to the exterior cellar doors, two heavy wooden doors that opened up and out and which were always left unlocked. I quietly pulled one of them open and quickly crept down the old cement steps into the basement. A light switch was immediately to my right as I reached the bottom of the steps. This I knew from my many trips to the cellar for jars of Sarah's preserves or canned vegetables. I decided against a light and slowly and carefully moved toward the stairs leading up to the kitchen. There was just enough light from upstairs to allow me to make out vague shapes. Even so, I carefully planted one foot in front of the other as I moved toward the light. Up above, the floor squeaked and groaned as the man moved about. I zigzagged my way, avoiding objects that blocked my path until I reached the stairs. I then slowly climbed the stairs, walking on the outer edges of the steps and skipping every other one to lessen the odds of making a sound. As I neared the kitchen, I raised the ax over my shoulders, preparing to swing the instant I stepped out into the kitchen. I wondered how much good the element of surprise would be against a maniacal killer with a gun. At the top of the steps, I paused briefly to prepare myself, picturing in my mind what I was going to do, and then I suddenly leapt out into the kitchen.

Sarah, screamed when she saw me. She was sitting at the table and jumped up, knocking her chair to the floor with a loud bang that echoed throughout the kitchen. With horror on her face, she slowly backed away from the table. The man, who had his back toward me, started to turn.

"Don't move!" I ordered in a voice that sounded a lot more unsure than I had intended, like Gilligan trying to sound like Rockford. For some reason, Sarah stopped quickly. The man continued to move.

"I said don't move! And keep your hands where I can see them!"

The red-faced man continued to turn until he caught sight of the ax raised above my head. He then carefully placed his hands on the table.

"Martin!" Sarah yelled. "What are you doing?"

Her arms too were raised in the air. The fear on her face was mingled with one of disbelief. Diane, who had probably been upstairs in bed all this time, ran into the kitchen, her flimsy nightgown barely covering her. She stopped suddenly at the sight of Sarah standing with her hands raised.

"Sarah, what's going on?" she asked.

As Diane turned her head, she saw me standing at the basement door with an ax at the ready.

"Martin, don't!" she screamed. "That's my dad!"

Dad? The red-faced man was her father? I was standing over him ready to kill him. In fact, it probably looked like I was going to kill all of them. For all they knew I had murdered Nick and Ted and was here to finish off the rest of the family.

I slowly lowered the ax to the floor and walked toward Sarah and Diane.

"I'm sorry. I thought . . ."

I didn't see the red-faced man move from his chair but I felt the man's shoulder as it slammed against me. He threw me to the hard oak floor, landing on top of me with all his weight. His clenched fist flew at me from the side, catching me hard on the jaw. I could taste blood as I turned to face my attacker, wanting to explain that this was all a mistake. I saw the glint of light reflect off the blade of a butcher knife that I could only assume had been lying on the table the whole time. Its cold steel came to rest against my neck, the razor-sharp edge nipping at the skin above my Adam's apple. I held my breath, knowing that swallowing now would cause me to slice my own throat. Angry eyes glared down at me as I looked up at the now even redder face.

"Nobody takes a fuckin' ax to me, fucker!" the red-faced man snarled as he held me down with his heavy, tattooed arm.

I wondered now if I had miscalculated again. Dad could still possibly be the killer. I'd had him at a disadvantage and let him get away.

"Lester, get off him!" Sarah cried. "Goddammit! Get off!"

"Stop it, Dad," Diane cried as her long, naked legs and scantily clad ass moved into my view. If I was going to die, I would happily carry that vision to eternity.

Reluctantly, Lester moved the knife from my throat. He ceased his attack and Diane led him back to his chair at the table.

Diane then sat on the floor and cradled my head into her lap, much as Ma Doherty had done a few hours earlier. The back of my neck rested against the smooth, cool skin of her thighs. She bent over and with soft moist lips, kissed the cheek which had just met with her father's fist. Without a doubt, Diane was much better at this than Ma Doherty.

Chapter 14

Diane's father glared at me from across the table as we sat drinking coffee. Even after Lester explained that he was just concerned about his daughter's safety, his mood toward me had not softened. Nor mine for him. His explanation that he was just hunting for a match when I had spotted him searching through Diane's purse didn't sit too well with me either. The old-fashioned matchbox holder, which he said he hadn't seen, hung in plain sight above the kitchen sink.

"I don't need to answer to you!" Lester finally shouted. "I ain't the one who came in here wielding an ax!"

"Maybe he just figured you didn't belong here," Sarah answered. I knew that Sarah had never cared much for Diane's father to begin with. She hated him for taking off and leaving Diane and her mother. The only reason Lester would be welcome in Sarah's house was if Diane had insisted.

Suddenly, Diane started laughing. It was a tiny laugh at first. It was a laugh she tried to suppress, until she just had to let it out.

"It *is* kind of funny you know," she managed to say in between laughing jags. "It looked like a scene from "Friday the Thirteenth" or something. Martin, if I didn't know better, I would have thought you were the crazed killer."

"What makes you think he isn't?" Lester growled.

"Because I *do* know better," Diane answered.

*   *   *

Diane and I sat at the kitchen table after Lester and Sarah went off to bed. We went through two pots of coffee as we discussed my encounter with the Doherty boys. Time had passed so quickly. I hadn't noticed it was almost three in the morning. Even though I was due at the post office in a few hours, I wasn't concerned. Sleep I could get any time. Diane was a different story. Her gentle hands reached across the table to caress my hand as she smiled at me angelically, a smile that almost made me forget the events of the last two days. In the soft kitchen light, she looked so innocent. I wondered how I could have even considered her a possible suspect in the murder of her uncles.

"I don't think you should rule out the Doherty brothers," Diane said.

"I'm not ruling anyone out yet."

The smile left her face as she contemplated my last statement.

"Did you pick up that envelope I told you about at the post office?" I continued.

"I tried but that fat guy . . . what's his name?"

"Ike."

"Yeah. Ike. He said that my father would have to pick it up."

"Your father! What's Lester got to do with it?" I asked.

"Everything. He's the executor of my uncles' wills."

Chapter 15

There appeared to be no one at the post office when I arrived there two hours earlier than usual. Ike's parking spot was vacant and all the interior lights of the building were off.

I parked my car around back out of sight and found my flashlight in the cluttered glove compartment. I stepped across the dew-covered grass toward the post office. I glanced eastward toward the Castle Rock Feed Mill. From the slight hint of light on the horizon, I guessed that the sun was still an hour away from rising. When I reached the front door of the post office, I fumbled with my keys and attempted to find the one that would turn the lock. I was about halfway through my collection of keys when a car turned on to Main Street, thundering its way toward me. I jumped down off the steps and hid behind a thick barberry bush, scratching the side of my face on its prickly branches. I don't know why I was so worried, because no one would consider my presence there unusual. Not even Sheriff Trout would arrest a guy for going to work early.

The car driven by Spunky, the town garbage man, probably on his way to work, headed toward the outskirts of town. I slinked out from behind the bush and, forgetting which keys I had already tried, started over again until I found the one that opened the front door.

I quickly closed the door behind me and turned on the flashlight. The beam of light cut a path in the hallway ahead as I slowly moved toward the back of the building. Shadows from bags of mail crept along the walls and faded into the darkness behind.

As I neared Ike's office, I was disappointed to see the door closed. My whole purpose for sneaking in early was to find the large brown envelope. I wanted to examine it before Lester got his hands on it. If it was the one I had delivered to the Novaceks, its contents might give me an idea why they were killed. If it was a bogus envelope, it would indicate that the real envelope was involved with their death. I could only hope that Ike was not one to lock his door.

Unfortunately, he was. I flashed my light in through the office window. I could see the large picture on the far wall of Ike's championship football team and a smaller family portrait below it. The envelope was not on his desk. The tops of filing cabinets and shelves were covered with books and manuals but no brown envelope. It was probably in one of the desk drawers, hopefully an unlocked desk drawer.

I firmly grabbed the handle and pushed at the door. Nothing. Ike had locked his door. Breaking the office window and reaching in to turn the lock was an option. It was a large window, about four by six feet, and its breaking would have to be explained. Preferably not by me. Nevertheless, I searched for something with which to smash the window. A sturdy, oak chair in the hallway seemed a likely candidate. Holding the chair in one hand and the flashlight in the other, I slammed the chair toward the target. However, it wasn't a direct hit. The chair glanced off leaving the window intact.

I was ready to throw the base of the chair at the window again when I noticed that the door to an adjoining office was ajar. The window was spared, at least for the moment. I checked the adjacent office for a possible means of entering Ike's office. There were no vents that I could remove. But the partition between the two offices didn't quite reach the ceiling. It looked like I might be able to access Ike's office through the opening. I just hope it was wide enough.

After sliding a desk over to the partition, I set a chair on top of the desk. I was then able to climb my improvised staircase and vault up and through the narrow opening. Unable to gauge the distance in the darkness, I crashed to the floor of Ike's office with a heavy thud. I was cursing myself for forgetting my flashlight in the other office when I heard the sound of a car door slam in the parking lot.

I crouched down to avoid being seen. I could hear footsteps outside the building approaching the front door.

I searched the office to find a possible hiding place. The coat rack would have been a possibility only if Ike's oversized coat were already hung on it. The filing cabinets were neither tall enough nor wide enough.

The sound of footsteps stopped as I heard the front door open. There was only one place left. Without making a sound, I scooted along the floor and crammed underneath Ike's desk. Years of wear and tear from Ike's shoes had worn two footprints in the tile, a perfect fit for the two cheeks of my buttocks. As I shifted to find a more comfortable position, my head grazed the bottom of the desktop. Something pulled the hair at the top of my head. Feeling above me, I discovered the cause of the pull. Gum. Ike had obviously not learned in school that the place for used gum was not under the desk. As I freed my hair from the gum, I banged the side of my head on Ike's desk. Surely, Ike or whoever it was had heard it. I waited in silence as the sound of footsteps moved toward Ike's office.

I could only hope that it wasn't Ike. And if it were, that he wouldn't sit down. There certainly wasn't enough room under the desk for me and Ike's fat legs. There was no way I could explain my presence under his desk. And knowing the sheriff, I figured Trout would be more than happy to arrest me. Even if he didn't, it would surely mean the loss of my job. Since no one in Castle Rock would ever hire me, I would have to leave the town I had grown to love.

The footsteps came to a stop at the door of Ike's office. For what seemed like minutes, everything was silent. Then the doorknob jiggled. It startled me, even though I had been expecting it.

"Martin! Are you in there?" someone whispered. A female voice. Only one person knew I was coming here.

I slid out from under the desk and looked out the office window. There stood Diane. She was leaning up against the window, her hands cupping her eyes as she peered in. When she spotted me, she waved her arms excitedly.

"I thought I heard you in there," she whispered.

"What the hell are you doing here?" I asked in a loud voice that seemed much louder with all the whispering going on.

"Come on. Let me in."

There wasn't much else to do but open the door for her. She was certainly dressed the part, all in black. Black hat, shoes, slacks, coat, and gloves that made the white of her face even whiter in contrast.

"Did you find it yet?" she asked as she slipped into the office.

I shook my head.

"Are you sure it's in here?"

Again, I shook my head. For all I knew, Ike had taken it home with him. Or locked it up in the Post Office safe. I was counting on Ike to be his usual lazy self and to do as little as possible.

After putting the adjoining room back in order, I joined Diane in the search of Ike's office. She had already looked in the desk and was now going through filing cabinets. I checked the shelves and bookcases. Nothing. It appeared that I had led us on a wild goose chase.

"My dad will get the envelope later this morning. Then we'll know what's in it," she said as she leaned against the desk.

"Maybe not," I answered as I began searching Ike's desk again.

"I already looked there," Diane said impatiently.

"You might have missed something."

When I looked up at her face, I saw an anger that I hadn't seen in her before. She was probably upset that I thought she had overlooked something.

Suddenly, the front door of the post office slammed. Again footsteps, loud and fast, moved toward us. I knew there was no way to avoid being discovered. I grabbed Diane, who'd already started for the door. I plopped down into Ike's office chair and pulled Diane onto my lap. Diane picked up the cue and put her arms around my neck. We kissed each other with all the passion of two people in love, a deep and powerful kiss that contained all the emotion of the last few days.

"Don't you have a home, Prescott?" Ike's voice boomed throughout the office. "And what the hell are you doing in my office?"

"Has it been so long ago you can't remember?" I asked, reluctantly separating myself from Diane. "Besides, you should lock your door if you want privacy."

"You know she isn't supposed to be in here," Ike fired back. "I could have you canned for this."

"I was just leaving," Diane said. She got up off my lap, picked up her purse, and headed out the door.

As I followed her out and started for the mailroom to begin work, I couldn't help noticing Diane's purse. Was it stuffed with something besides the usual female items? Or was I just imagining things?

Chapter 16

The farm across the road from the Novaceks belonged to a reclusive widower named Alfred Barton. I figured that it might be a good idea to ask Alfred if he had noticed anything that might help us. As Diane and I drove down the long, seldom-traveled driveway toward his farmhouse, I wondered what he looked like, since I had never met him. Alfred never got any mail; he didn't even have a mailbox. From the stories I had heard, Alfred was a fat, tall, skinny, short, bald man with long, white hair who had killed his sixty-year-old teenage wife with a twelve-gauge, semi-automatic, double-bladed chain saw. This much was told to me as fact. The rest is speculation. That Alfred had organized a secret cult that met weekly in his barn. That Alfred was really an undercover FBI agent. That Alfred was most likely dead.

The latter proved not to be true. If Alfred noticed us as we approached, he showed no sign of it. In fact, he seemed more intent on what he was doing. Whittling. Even when we came to a stop within a few feet of him, it was as if we were not there at all.

A tattered straw hat barely covered his bald head. His soiled work shirt and overalls strained to hold in his short, fat frame. If they were indeed his clothes, they had outgrown their usefulness about thirty pounds and thirty years ago.

The slamming of the car doors echoed over the quiet farmyard. That also drew no response from Alfred.

"Hello, Alfred," I said.

Alfred continued whittling away.

"Alfred!" I yelled louder.

"This is getting us nowhere," Diane finally said when there was no answer. "Absolutely nowhere."

"That's for sure. Hell, he can't even tell we're standing right in front of him. How could he know what went on over at Nick and Ted's place?"

"It's too bad," Diane responded as she looked through a gap in the dense trees toward the Novacek farm. "You can get a good view of the place from here."

I glanced over toward the Novaceks' farm also. It appeared so calm and peaceful I almost expected to see Nick and Ted appear at a doorway at any second.

"Is that all he does?" Diane asked.

"Must be," I answered. "Judging from the pile of chips on the ground."

Alfred didn't appear to be carving anything in particular. At least that I could figure out. Just making a large piece of wood into a small one.

"It's strange though," I continued. "From the looks of this place, he must do some work around here, sometime."

The buildings were all kept up and appeared to have been recently painted. The grass was mowed and trimmed and a large, well-manicured garden occupied the space between the house and garage.

I was almost starting to buy into the cult story and that perhaps Alfred had slipped into some sort of meditational trance. However, from the looks of Alfred, I thought the theory that Alfred was dead was also a possibility. I wondered if I could even rule out Alfred's being an undercover FBI man.

"Well, we might as well go," I finally said. "We've found out all we're going to here."

We turned toward the car and stopped abruptly. I was staring into the barrel of a shotgun held by a tall, thin man with long, flowing blonde hair.

"The sign says no trespassing," the man growled. "But since you're the mailman, it don't surprise me none that you can't read."

"I didn't see any sign," I nervously answered.

"There wasn't any sign," Diane boldly said.

"Damn it. Don't tell me there wasn't any sign."

"Well, there wasn't," Diane said again.

"Listen. I got the damn gun. And I say there was a sign," he yelled. He turned the gun toward Diane and then back on me. "What the hell you doin' over here now? Are you through raising hell over at the Novacek place and you want to pull the same shit here?"

"Actually, we were wondering if Alfred there could help us."

A huge laugh shook his entire frame.

"That man ain't Alfred and he can't help you. And who the hell is Alfred?"

"Alfred Barton. The guy who owns this place," I answered.

"That's not Alfred Barton. That's Fred Denison. My crazy brother-in-law. Been that way ever since his sister, my wife, died. Come to think of it, he wasn't much different before."

"And you must be Al Barton," I said.

"Bingo."

Al menacingly waved the gun at me.

"Now you two got just thirty seconds to get off my place."

"Sure. No problem," I said as Diane and I slowly stepped back toward the car. "You sure keep a good eye on this place. You ever notice anything that goes on at the Nick and Ted's?"

"Hell, I know most everything that goes on over there."

"Even on the day Nick and Ted were killed?"

"Sure as hell do. Even saw you over there snooping around."

"Did you notice anything strange over there that day?"

"Other than you crawling in windows, no. Now get the hell out of here."

I quickly got into my car and slammed the door. Through my open window I asked one more question.

"Did you notice anyone else over there that day?"

"No. Nobody unusual. Only other person out there that morning was Trout."

Chapter 17

The rest of the day, I went through the motions of delivering mail. A day that seemed to drag on partly because I'd had no sleep the night before, and partly because I would rather have been solving the murder. It had become an obsession. I tried to piece things together in my mind, wondering if I was leaving out some important and obvious fact, or making too much of something that might have nothing to do with the killings. The large brown envelope, for example. And I had to wonder what part Diane played in all of this. Her actions sure seemed suspicious. I hoped I was wrong and that she was not hiding anything from me.

I deposited a *Lutheran Brotherhood* magazine into Mrs. Olander's mailbox, another of the interesting mailboxes on my route. Hers looked like a miniature covered wagon. Others on the route resembled milk trucks, barns, old threshing machines, John Deere tractors, and outhouses. Mr. Freuder's cow-box was the one that bothered me the most. Its rear end stuck out toward the road. Having to lift the cow's tail to open the box always made me feel more like a veterinarian than a mailman. However, my favorite was a quite ordinary-looking mailbox that belonged to George Hendry. Its unique feature was that it couldn't be knocked down. Four heavy-duty springs attached near the base allowed it to bend but not break. High school kids, drunks, hay wagons and even school buses had taken their best shots at it over the years, but with no success.

Mrs. Olander was also the last delivery of the day for me. I headed back toward town, driving faster than usual, leaving a giant dust trail behind me. Rocks from the gravel road peppered the bottom of my car.

As I passed the Novacek farm, I glanced over, almost expecting to see Nick and Ted waving to me from their yard. Instead, I caught sight of a vehicle parked behind the house, as if in a failed attempt to conceal its presence from the road. I slowed down past the driveway, backed up, and decided to check. I started down the Novacek driveway. I drove slowly, careful not to race my engine and careful not to alert whoever it was that was snooping around the place. My car bounced from one deep rut to another, ruts that had gotten deeper since Nick and Ted were killed. Weeds were already escaping from the ditch, eager to overtake the driveway.

The sound filled the car first. An explosion. Like a cherry bomb had ignited inside the car. Then, the sound of glass shattering. Glass from the windshield on the passenger side rained into the front seat. I slammed on the brakes and ducked down. Craning my head upward, I saw the softball-size hole in the glass. It had to be a warning shot, didn't it? Whoever shot had to know that I was driving a mail car and therefore on the right side of the car. Or was it meant to kill? Was I fortunate to be alive at this moment?

I was breathing quickly and my heart was beating rapidly. I listened for any noise outside as I wondered what to do next. I was sure that if I stuck my head up to see what was going on, another more accurate shot would hit me. If I stayed where I was, I'd be a sitting duck for whoever was trying to kill me. I opened my door. I could see trees across the alfalfa field. I could make a run for them, but I would have to run about a hundred yards before I would be assured of cover. Instead, I put the car in reverse and pressed my foot down on the accelerator. The car snaked its way backward as I tried to steer with my face only about two feet above the road. The car had only gone about five yards when another shot exploded into the windshield, this time on the steering wheel side.

Glass showered onto my hair and down my shirt. The bullet had ripped a hole in the headrest where my head would normally be. I pressed down harder on the accelerator, making it more difficult to guide the car backward down the road. Weeds slapped up against my face when I got too close to the ditch, temporarily blinding me until I turned the steering wheel. The car suddenly leaned down away from me, which meant I was headed into the opposite ditch. Adjusting the wheel again, I made my way toward the end of the driveway. Another shot crashed against the windshield, this one clipping off the rear view mirror.

Finally, I reached the end of the driveway and backed out onto the county road, making sure to keep my side away from the direction of the house. The car slid across the gravel road and dropped into the ditch on the far side of the road, ripping the door off its hinges. My seat belt clamped me firmly to the seat, preventing me from being thrown out of the car, possibly underneath it.

When the car came to a stop, I hung loosely from the seat belt, the tilted car attempting to dump me in the weeds below. I reached back and unsnapped the belt. More quickly then I expected, I found myself ejected from the car, landing face first in what seemed like a soft pile of weeds. When my hands struck the ground, I felt the burning pain of gravel scraping across my palms. Then the darkness swept over me as I passed out.

Chapter 18

A voice.

That was the next sound I heard. I was still in the ditch. I had no idea how long I had been out. It could have been minutes, hours, or days for all I knew.

I turned my head uncomfortably toward the direction of the voice. A familiar voice. A painfully familiar voice. I squinted out of the darkness. The light pierced through my slitted eyelids. A sharp stab of pain raced from my eyes and slammed against the back of my head. I peered foggily out of the weeds toward the mountainous figure of Sheriff Trout standing on the road above me. I wondered why Trout didn't come down into the ditch to help me. But if Trout did crawl down into the ditch, he'd probably never be able to get back out again. Not without a tow truck anyway. Was it laughter I heard as I struggled to get to my knees? Again, a darkness swept over me. Something soft and moist touched my face. Smooth lips kissing my cheeks. Surely not Trout's, I hoped. I again squinted my eyes open, relieved to find Diane leaning over me. This was beginning to become a habit, although one which I could easily get used to.

"Thank God you're all right."

I closed my eyes and enjoyed the loving attention Diane was giving me. If only I didn't have to get beat up or almost killed to receive it.

"You are all right, aren't you?" Diane asked.

"Yes, I think so," I answered as I sat up slowly. I opened my eyes wider and looked into Diane's beautiful blue eyes, eyes that were showing so much concern for me.

"I'll be okay." I winced. My head ached from the bump on the back of head. Diane pulled my head to her breasts, tenderly caressing my head until the hurting subsided.

"You really scared the hell out of me," Diane said. "Finding you in the ditch like this. I didn't know if you were dead or alive."

I reluctantly pulled myself from Diane's arms.

"Where's Sheriff Trout?" I asked.

"Trout?" There was a look of puzzlement on Diane's face. I slowly turned and looked up to the side of the road for Trout.

"Isn't Sheriff Trout here?" I asked.

"I haven't seen him," Diane answered. "And if he were here, there's no way I could have missed him."

I was really confused now. Had Trout actually been here? Or had I only imagined it all? A hallucination caused by the blow to my head? If so, it was a strange image to conjure up. And why? I figured Trout would be the last person I would dream about.

I lifted my left wrist to look at my Timex. I wanted to check how long I'd been out. My eyes still were not clear. The numbers on my watch were nothing more than a blur.

"Diane, what time is it?"

"Three-thirty," she answered, after checking her watch.

How long had the shooting incident taken? I tried to run through it again in my mind. The events seemed to pass by in slow motion and fast-forward at the same time. I could only guess it took minutes. Five at the most. So I estimated that I had lain in the ditch for about fifteen minutes. Surely enough time for Trout to come by and then abandon me before Diane arrived.

I got to my knees and started to crawl out of the ditch.

"Here," Diane offered. "Let me help you."

She put my arm around her neck and lifted upward.

I placed my weight on her shoulders. As we crawled from the ditch, I was surprised at how strong she was. It seemed like she was almost carrying me out.

"I work out at the club," she said, sensing the question before I could ask it. "Lift weights and work the Nautilus."

That figures, I thought.

When we reached the road, I slowly got to my feet, my legs wobbling beneath me. The blood rushing to my legs made me dizzy, causing me to lean on Diane again. She didn't seem to mind.

I scanned the gravel road for footprints and tire tracks. I found plenty of each, but there was no way to tell when they had been made.

"Martin!" Diane cried out. She had moved to the front of the car and was examining the shattered windshield. "Someone was shooting at you. Who was it?"

"That's what I'd like to know," I answered. "Did you see anybody at all when you got here? Any cars or trucks?"

"No. But after I saw your car in the ditch I probably wouldn't have noticed anything else."

"What are you doing out here?" I asked. "Did you know I was here?"

"No. I'm supposed to meet my father. He called to say he had picked up the envelope and asked me to meet him out here."

"The envelope? Did he say what was in it?"

"No. He just said he couldn't talk about it over the phone," Diane said. "Come on. Let's go up to the house. Maybe my father is there now."

"No, wait!" I demanded. "That's where the shots came from. Whoever shot at me might still be there."

"Whoever it was is probably gone by now. Could be he was only trying to chase you off."

"Could be it worked," I said.

"Ah, you're just being scaranoid again."

"Scaranoid, hell! Look at my windshield. I have reason to be scared. Someone was trying to kill me!"

A plume of dust appeared down the gravel road. I could hear the siren approaching, getting louder and louder as it neared us. The flashing red lights of the sheriff's car appeared over the horizon. Even from a mile away, I could see the car lean to one side from the weight of Sheriff Trout.

Finally the car neared the Novacek driveway and skidded to a stop next to Diane and me. Trout's face peered out of the window at us.

"Figured you'd be okay," he said.

"Then you were here earlier?" I asked.

"Saw you coming out of it earlier. Would've helped you but I took off after the guy that shot at you. He left here like a bat outta hell. Would've caught him too, but he had a head start on me."

It didn't surprise me at all that Trout could lose my attacker, even with the help of a dust trail.

"Did you see who it was?" I asked.

"Hell, I couldn't see anything with the dust and all," Trout answered. He turned and stared at Diane, his eyes riveted on her breasts. Diane, who previously had shown no signs of modesty, crossed her arms in front her and uncomfortably turned away.

"Looks like you don't need me anymore. Best be getting back to town," Trout announced.

"But aren't you going to look around the farmhouse?" I asked.

"No need to do that. Whoever was there is long gone."

With that, he rolled his window up and gunned his engine, spinning his wheels. Gravel flew back toward Diane and me as Trout fishtailed down the dirt road.

"What an asshole!" Diane screamed as she turned away from the flying rocks. "I thought people quit doing that shit when they got out of high school."

"He probably watches too many police shows on television. Probably thinks he's Robocop or something," I said. I looked toward the farmhouse, cupping my eyes to shield them from the setting sun. Everything looked peaceful enough, causing me to wonder if I had just imagined the shots coming from the house. I was still in a fog after the bump on the head. My ears were ringing and squinting into the sun caused me to wince.

"Maybe we should get you to a doctor," Diane said.

"That can wait. Right now, let's go check out that farmhouse."

"All right." Diane said. She ran to her car, jumped in, and reached over to open the passenger door for me.

I slowly walked to the car, my legs still unsure beneath me. Out of nowhere, a dusty orange school bus slowed to a crawl next to me. Thirty kids with their faces pressed against the windows looked excitedly at my car lying on its side in the ditch. The driver, Bruce, opened his window and yelled out.

"What happened, Prescott? A mailbox get the best of you?"

I didn't figure that deserved an answer.

"Want me to pull you out?"

"Just have Ike send a tow truck out," I answered.

Bruce nodded and drove off, leaving me to wonder what had actually happened.

Chapter 19

After I got in the car, I had Diane drive to the place on the county road from where I had spotted the car hidden behind the house. The car was gone.

"What was that all about?" Diane asked as she headed back to the Novacek driveway.

"I just don't want us to drive into what I did last time."

"Sheriff Trout said the guy took off," Diane said.

"I never did believe much of what Trout had to say before. Now, I don't believe anything."

The short trip down the driveway seemed to last an eternity. My mind flashed back to what had happened just minutes ago. I envisioned another shot blasting its way into the car. Looking over to where Diane was sitting behind the steering wheel, I suddenly appreciated the fact that I drove the mail car with its steering wheel on the right side. If it had been in the normal position, I probably wouldn't be alive now.

The first shot could have been a warning from someone who knew I drove a mail car. But then why the other shots after I had already started my retreat? They were obviously meant to kill me. And once I had landed unconscious in the ditch, the attacker would have had no trouble killing me in the ditch. Sheriff Trout had probably prevented that from occurring when he had happened by the first time. As much as I hated to admit it, and as much Trout would like to see me dead, Trout had probably saved my life. Unintentionally, of course.

"I wonder why my dad isn't here yet!" Diane asked as we neared the farmhouse.

"Maybe he already was," I answered, wondering if I should have voiced my suspicion.

Diane turned angrily toward me.

"Hey, my dad wouldn't have done this to you!"

"How do you know? You don't know him. You just met him yesterday!"

"Why would he shoot you? What reason would he have?"

Diane came to a stop in front of the farmhouse, quickly got out of the car, and ran to the front door. The plywood that had covered the door had been completely pulled down. I summoned all the little strength within me and caught up with her just as she was about to enter.

"Let's go in together this time," I demanded.

Diane nodded in agreement. We crossed the threshold. The unmistakable odor of gunpowder greeted us. That made sense. The shots fired at me had come from inside the house.

When my eyes became accustomed to the darkness inside the house, I saw that the place had been practically gutted. Almost all the plaster on the living room walls had been torn down, leaving just the grids of slats. What had one once been the Novacek living room wall formed a giant pile on the living floor.

"What the hell!" Diane exclaimed. She picked up a big hunk of plaster and inspected it as if it might give her some clue of what had happened. "Do you think it could have been vandals?"

"Maybe," I answered. "Or some partying teenagers out to have a good time." I remembered trashing an abandoned house with a group of my friends when still in high school. We had enjoyed the thrill of breaking windows, knowing there would be no recriminations. Pulling doors off their hinges. Even throwing an old dresser through a second-story window and watching it reduced to kindling when it splintered on impact with the ground.

But upon closer examination, I noticed that this destruction seemed more deliberate. Not all the plaster had been torn from the walls, just certain sections. In some places, the walls were untouched; pictures and calendars hung askew from their hooks. In some places, it looked like a sledgehammer had broken through the wall, to spaces where only mice had traveled before.

"It seems like there was a method to their madness," I said, pointing to lines drawn in pencil upon the wall. "And for the most part, they even stayed inside the lines."

"They?" Diane asked. "How do you know there was more than one person?"

"I don't," I answered truthfully. In fact, I had always thought of the Novaceks' killer as one person, and my assailant as that very same person. Why I had suddenly switched to more than one killer puzzled even myself.

"It just looks like it would take more than one person to do this," I said.

Diane impatiently looked at her watch. "I wonder why my dad isn't here yet."

"Maybe he isn't coming."

"Of course he's coming. At least, I think he is. He said he'd meet me here."

She moved over toward a window, pulling the old, dirty curtains aside. Sunlight poured through the window, brightly illuminating the living room and casting Diane's long shadow on the floor behind her. I stared at her shapely leg as it escaped from the slit on the side of her skirt. She turned to face me.

"Martin! What are you staring at?"

My eyes had become riveted on Diane's feet. Diane looked down as well. There was a dark footprint where her shoe had been.

We trailed the red footprints back to the pile of debris in the center of the living room, to the pool of red blood next to it. A pool that was growing larger with the blood oozing from beneath the pile.

I knelt next to the pile and began removing pieces of plaster. To my astonishment, I was joined by Diane, who feverishly dug into the pile.

"Wait. Are you sure you want to do this?"

"You mean it could be my father. I know. But I've got to find out!"

She continued to tear at the debris. I didn't think I would be able to do it. If there was any chance that my father might be dead at the bottom of the pile, I wouldn't want to uncover him. Maybe because I hated my father and never wanted to see him again.

"Aayee!"

Diane's scream echoed through the living room as she jumped back. I looked to see a hand protruding from the heap. A hand caked with globs of red, blood-soaked plaster. I looked at Diane who knelt, holding her own now-scarlet hands in front of her. After a few seconds, she resumed her search into the pile. I slid over next to her and helped, uncovering a man's elbow and back; Diane was digging where the head would be located. Gradually, hair appeared. Gray or white hair. Maybe dark hair just white with dust. I stopped and watched as Diane carefully cleared the plaster from the man's face.

"Martin," Diane screamed. "It's not him!"

I looked closely and had to agree. Strange, but I felt disappointed. Deep inside I almost wanted it to be Lester.

"Then who is it?" Diane asked. "Do you know him?"

"I think so."

I reached down and gently turned the head further to make sure. When I was sure, I really wished that it had been Diane's father.

"It's Earl," I said. "Why would anyone want to kill him?"

"Who's Earl?" Diane asked.

"Just a harmless old drunk. At least he appeared to be. What would he be doing out here anyway? I've never known him to be this far away from a drink before."

"I could use one myself right now," Diane said. She slowly got up, wiping her bloodstained hands on a white handkerchief.

"Looks like I caught you. Red-handed, you might say."

Sheriff Trout's voice filled the room. His body was silhouetted against the doorway, blocking out all light from outside.

"Trying to cover up the body, I see."

"No," Diane answered. "He was dead when we got here."

"Well, Prescott. Seems like this is getting to be a habit with you. What is it with you and this house and dead bodies?"

Trout waddled over to me, reaching behind and pulling out a pair of handcuffs from his belt.

"I kind of figured it was you all along. I was just waiting for you to trip yourself up."

With that, he clamped the cuffs securely on my wrists.

"You can't arrest him," Diane yelled. "He hasn't done anything."

"Since when has that made any difference to Trout?" I said.

Chapter 20

Jail. I had never been in jail before. It was a lot like I had imagined it, though. The cots were uncomfortable; the toilet bowl in the middle of the back wall of the cell was crusted with urine. The walls were filled with graffiti, even the standard marks ticking off the days. Fortunately, I had a cell to myself. I had expected Trout to throw me in a cell with a grotesque hulk of a man who would make my life a living hell, torturing me at his leisure. Apparently, Trout was unable to find such a man. Therefore, he had to do it himself.

He had starved me, not feeding me until noon the next day. And then it was just an old crusty bologna sandwich and a carton of warm, slightly souring milk. Meanwhile, Trout sat directly outside the cell gorging himself on an entire fried chicken, a large platter of mashed potatoes with gravy, a dozen biscuits, three cobs of corn, a half gallon of Kemp's chocolate ice cream, all washed down by a six-pack of Schmidt Beer. He was actually doing me a favor. After watching Trout gulp down his food, I had lost my appetite. He reminded me of Novaceks' hogs at slopping time, especially when he chomped on the ears of corn, dibbling most of the kernels down the front of his shirt and onto the floor. I pushed the uneaten sandwich and full carton of milk back out of the cell.

"Not hungry, Prescott?" Trout grunted in between bites. "You best eat. A dying man needs to keep up all the strength he can."

"What the hell does that mean?" I asked. "It sounds like something you heard on an old Gunsmoke rerun."

Trout angrily tossed the cob of corn down on to his plate and pushed his tray away. I didn't think anything would cause Trout to do that. Trout stood up and walked over and pressed his face against the bars, spitting out tiny chunks of chicken and corn as he spoke.

"Goddammit, Prescott, you are a cocky bastard. Let's see how smart you are when the judge puts you away for the rest of your chicken-shit life."

"What happened to your theory of Nick and Ted's murder-suicide?"

"That's where I got you, Prescott. That was just to set you up and you fell for it. I knew sooner or later you'd trip yourself up. I just didn't think you'd do it in as grand a style as you did. Killing Earl like that and all."

"Now why would I want to kill Nick and Ted?" I asked. "They're about the only friends I had in this whole town."

"That's just it," Trout sputtered. "They confided in you. Probably told you where they had their money stashed."

"What money?" I asked.

"The two million dollars," Trout answered as a matter of fact. The Novaceks' fortune, if there was one, grew larger every day.

"I don't know what you did with it," Trout continued, "but that's why you killed the Novaceks. Then, to throw me off the track, you called me, pretending to have discovered the bodies."

"Why didn't you just arrest me then?"

"I knew I didn't have enough to hold you on," he replied. "But you knew I was on to you. Damn right you did. That's why you been snooping around, even all the way to Little

Chicago, trying to find someone else to pin it on. But I didn't fall for it. Not for a second."

"And Earl?" I asked.

"He knew too much," Trout answered. "Somehow he found out about you. Maybe even where you hid the money. In the walls, I figure. And when he went out there to get it, you caught him tearing down the walls. Naturally you had to shut him up. And that's where I got you."

"I can see where it makes sense. To you," I said. "But it's not the way it happened."

"Oh, it's what happened all right."

"I see it more like this," I said. "You know who killed the Novaceks and you want to pin it on me. As long as you could pass it off as a murder-suicide, everything was fine. But when I started to hunt around to find out who really did it, the people who paid you off got nervous. Maybe even as early as the same day when I asked questions at the Crow Bar. Therefore, the trip through the country in your Sheriff's car until my house was ransacked and it was all right for me to come home."

"What the hell is this shit about your house being ransacked?" Trout asked. I couldn't tell if the puzzled expression on Trout's face was real or just for my benefit. "This is the first I've heard of it."

"That surprises me," I said. "When I got home that night, I was greeted by the living room from hell. Your boys did a great job on it."

"Listen, Prescott. My boys had nothing to do with it. They got better things to do. If your place was torn apart, it was probably by someone looking for the money you got from the Novaceks. I'm more convinced now than before you're guilty as hell."

"And Sheriff, I'm convinced that you know who's behind all this and you're covering it up. Maybe they have something on you and they're blackmailing you, or they're paying you, or it's a childhood friend you don't want to turn in. Either that or you're the stupidest, most incompetent sheriff in the whole country."

Trout's face turned an even brighter shade of red than I thought possible. He opened his mouth, trying to speak for what seemed like a minute, and nothing came out. Finally a barrage of expletives echoed throughout the jail. I had to admit; there was something Trout was good at, besides eating.

"If you think I'm so goddamned stupid," Trout said, "how come I'm out here free and your ass is locked in this jail?"

Trout had a point there.

Chapter 21

"Prescott! What the hell are you doing out?"

It wasn't the first time I had heard this question today. And I was afraid it wasn't going to be the last.

Howie Lentch draped an elbow over his mailbox for support as I handed him his mail. Howie examined it closely, as if he were looking for something that might not be there.

"This all of it?" he asked.

"Something missing?" I asked.

"Guess not. Didn't think they'd let you out yet, let alone deliver the mail."

"Someone bailed me out. I must have at least one friend. Hard to believe!"

"That you haven't killed off anyway. Yet," Howie answered as he headed to his farmyard without even a good-bye.

Everyone in Castle Rock had already tried and convicted me. They would probably have executed me by now if they could have. I was still an outsider to this town. Sure, I had grown to be accepted, but only marginally. Until now, when I had proved their initial suspicions correct.

I almost wished I were still in jail. During the week I had spent there, I had felt safe. But I had missed the Novaceks' funerals. And I had been forced to endure Sheriff Trout's harassment and ridicule. It was a unique form of torture, being confined to a cell and forced to listen to Trout constantly boast of his successful resolution of the Castle Rock Slayings.

I was relieved to be bailed out, thanks to Sarah, Diane, and a famous Minneapolis defense attorney, Albert Feeny, who Diane had brought in. According to Feeny, I had nothing to worry about, even though I had both the motive and opportunity. The opportunity was obvious. I had been found at both crime scenes. The motive was less obvious. And according to Trout, Diane was just someone who had happened to be in the wrong place at the wrong time.

The county prosecutor had already built a strong case against me. He was a close friend and classmate of Trout and Ike. He was also under extreme pressure to convict the murderer or murderers of Nick, Ted, and Earl. It didn't matter if it happened to be me, or that I was innocent.

But I did worry as I drove from Howie's farm to the Sintelar place a mile down the road. It wouldn't surprise me if the prosecutor could find a jury of locals who would find me guilty, regardless of whether or not they were friends of Trout. And even if Albert Feeny were to help me be acquitted, the people of Castle Rock would always believe I was guilty.

I spotted Margaret Sintelar standing across the road from her mailbox as I turned from County Road 6 on to County Road 21. As I deposited the mail, she stood and stared at me, guarding her three young children who hid behind her skirt.

No, if I was going to be free or have any chance to live in this town again, I would have to search for the real killer myself. And more earnestly than I had before. Prior to my arrest, my sleuthing had been like a game. Now, there was more at stake. And it would also be more difficult. The residents of Castle Rock were not likely to be very cooperative.

*   *   *

I had arranged to meet Diane at Sarah's after my route. When I arrived, she was anxiously waiting for me on the front porch. She ran out to greet me as I slowed to a stop under a giant elm.

"God, am I glad you're here. I was going nuts just sitting around. So what do we do now?"

"Any news from your father?" I asked.

"I haven't heard from him. And Sarah doesn't know where he is, either."

"The sonofabitching snake probably crawled back down the same hole he came out of," Sarah called out as she approached from the barn, empty pail in hand. "He's the one they should've arrested. Not Martin, here. Except he's probably two states away by now."

"Sarah! You don't know that," Diane answered.

"I reckon there's a lot of things I don't know that are true. Like there's lots of things you know that aren't. How come he didn't meet you at Nick and Ted's?"

"Maybe something happened to him," Diane said.

"We can only hope," Sarah said, as she turned for the house. "We can only hope!"

Chapter 22

As I cautiously drove down the long, narrow driveway leading to the Barton farmhouse, I wasn't so sure I wanted to go back there again. After all, we had been chased off the Barton farm at gunpoint the previous time. But now that I was a suspect, I decided that any information I might be able to obtain from Al Barton would be worth the risk. My shirt was thoroughly soaked, partly, I figured, from the heat and humidity of the late afternoon summer day and partly from the anxiety of revisiting Al Barton.

I glanced over toward Diane, who had insisted upon accompanying me. She sat relaxed in the seat next to me, gazing out over the freshly fertilized fields. Neither the pungent odor of the manure nor the prospect of facing Al Barton's shotgun again seemed to bother her.

"My God, don't you ever sweat?" I asked her.

She turned slowly toward me with a sexy smile etched on her lips.

"Sure," she answered. "When I'm horny."

I was startled by her comment. I had never known a woman as open as she was. From now on, I would keep an even more watchful eye on her. If she were ever to perspire, I surely wouldn't want to miss it.

She moved closer to me and wiped the beads of sweat from my face.

"You must be really horny," she laughed.

"Doesn't work that way with me," I responded, though I did seem to be sweating more now that Diane had moved closer, if that was possible.

It was then, despite driving as slow as I could without stopping, that I reached the Barton farmhouse. Al Barton was nowhere in sight and I was somewhat relieved. Although I needed to glean some information from him, I was ecstatic that I wasn't staring into the barrel of a shotgun again.

The silent Fred wasn't on the porch whittling, either. In fact the whole farm seemed deadly quiet. No dogs barked. I could hear no tractors on the fields. The sounds of all live-stock were absent.

"Where the hell is everybody?" Diane asked as she craned her neck out her open car window. "I thought they hardly ever left the place."

"Maybe they haven't," I answered. "This reminds me so much of your uncles' place. The day I found them."

"You don't think the same thing happened to them?"

"I don't know what to think any more."

"Maybe we should check inside," Diane offered.

"That's all I need," I said. "To be found at another mur-der scene. The whole town would probably lynch me. Sheriff Trout surely wouldn't try to stop them."

Against my better judgment, we got out of the car and started for the front door of the house. As we approached the steps, a groan emanated from under the porch. We stopped and squatted down to get a better look under the porch. Again the groan could be heard. Two arms and a head appeared between the bottom of the porch and the ground. With another loud groan, the entire person of Fred Denison squirted out.

I hurried over to help Fred, who was covered from head to toe with dark, black dirt.

"Are you okay? Were you hiding?"

"Not hiding. Why hide?"

"Then what were you doing under there?" Diane asked.

"Jeez, you're pretty," he finally said.

"Oh, thank you!" Diane answered, accepting the compliment that she'd probably heard a thousand times. "That's so nice of you to say."

I had to agree. She was beautiful and I hadn't even told her that.

Fred's eyes opened wide as he stared at Diane.

"Not you. Him," he said angrily as he pointed to me. "Jeez."

Diane looked stunned for an instant before the puzzled look left her face. She then had to bring a hand up to her face to conceal her laugh.

"Ah, thanks," I said not knowing where to go from there. No one had ever said that to me before. And it had to be Fred. Dirty, crazy Fred.

"Is Al around?" I asked to change the subject.

"You're talking to him. Alfred. Alfred Barton."

"But there is no Alfred Barton," I said. "Your brother-in-law said you were Fred Denison."

"Are you going to believe him? Jeez."

"Why not?"

We stood in silence for a few seconds as the warm breeze brought the pungent barnyard aroma up toward the house. Two chickens clucked their way down the yard to the chicken coup. Finally the dirty round man spoke again.

"He's crazy. Ever since my sister died. Won't let me talk. He still talks to her though. And he hears her too, I think. Jeez."

I glanced over at Diane. The look on my face must surely have matched the one on hers. I didn't know who or what to believe.

"Did you see anyone at the Novacek place the day they were murdered?"

"Yes," Alfred answered. "You. Jeez."

"Anyone else."

"Trout and his deputies and . . ."

The bullet seemed to pass within a hair of my ear before I heard the rifle shot and the bullet slam against a tree across the yard. I listened for the scream from Diane, but none came. I looked over to see that she was staring angrily at the tall, thin Barton.

"What the hell are you two doing back here? Seems to me I told you not to come back here."

"I just need some more information," I said. "And then we'll go."

"You'll go when I say you'll go. Now!"

He fired a shot past my other ear. I firmly held my ground as we stared into each other's eyes. Finally the gun lowered to the ground.

"What the hell's so damn important you want to get killed to know?"

"Before, you said Trout was at the farm the day the Novaceks were killed."

"Yeah, so what?"

"Was that before or after they were murdered?"

"What the hell you need to ask me that for? You should know as good as me. You were there when he got there."

"Shit," I said. "I guess we might as well go."

Diane and I slid into the car and started it up. Before we made it out of the yard, we heard the voice of the dirty Barton.

". . . and Sarah!"

Chapter 23

Our silence lasted only until we left the driveway.

"Did you hear what he said? Sarah was there," Diane said. "She never mentioned that to me. How about you, Martin?"

"Not to me," I answered. "But we don't know that she was. After all, we just have the word of a guy who spends his time playing in the dirt underneath his porch."

I wanted to believe that the dirty Barton was lying, that he was crazy. I didn't want to believe that Sarah was at the Novacek farm that morning or that she might have had something to do with their deaths.

"How well do you know Sarah?" Diane asked.

"Well enough," I answered.

Sarah had never lied to me before. At least that I knew. But she may not have had a reason to before.

"You don't seriously suspect Sarah, do you?" I asked.

"It's possible," Diane answered.

"Sure, anything is possible. But it doesn't seem likely," I said. "About the only people we're sure didn't kill the Novaceks are me and you. And I'm not so sure about you sometimes."

"And I'm not so sure about you either. You're the one they arrested," she pointed out.

"Hell, why should I kill them? What reason would I have?" I answered. "Unlike you, who had plenty of reason!"

"What about me?"

"Well, what about you?"

Diane angrily turned from me and stared out at the passing countryside. I drove silently, gripping the steering wheel tightly. Then, Diane buried her face in her hands and began to sob. Her entire body convulsed. I then wondered how I could have suspected her. I should have been grateful instead. If it weren't for her, I would be alone. Everyone else in Castle Rock would have nothing to do with me. But she had annoyed me and I had fought back with words harsh enough to bring her to tears.

"I'm sorry," I finally said.

Diane finally removed her hands from her face and turned to me. But there were no tears. Instead, Diane's face was contorted in a suppressed laugh. Her eyes and lips were forced shut. When she could hold it no longer, a breathy laugh escaped. She fanned her hands attempting to cool her face.

"I can't help it," she said. "But you've got to admit. It is pretty funny."

"Just what's so damn funny?" I flashed angrily.

"Us," Diane said. "We're really some kind of detectives. Instead of narrowing the suspects down, we keep coming up with more and more."

Finally I had to laugh. As furious at her as I was, she was right. And so damned cute. How could anyone stay mad at her?

"I guess you're right," I said. "Is there anyone in the whole state that we've eliminated?"

"Besides Nick and Ted themselves, no," Diane answered. "I wonder what the governor was doing that morning."

"What do you say we start crossing names off the list?" I suggested. "I'll start with you. I must admit at first I had some questions about you. But I don't believe that you would be capable of doing it."

"And I'll take your name off. If Trout thinks you did it, it must have been somebody else," Diane joked. "Besides, I believe you."

"Now, let's see if we can eliminate a few more suspects," I said. "Let's start with Sarah."

Chapter 24

Sarah's driveway appeared up ahead of us. It was going to be difficult. How would I bring up the subject?

"Is there something you've been wanting to tell me?"

Or, "What were you doing on the morning Nick and Ted were killed?"

Or, the direct approach: "Did you kill Nick and Ted?"

Sarah was feeding her chickens as we drove into her yard. She tossed grain to the right of her and the horde of chickens rushed in a feeding frenzy to her right. Then she tossed some grain to her left and the same hens ran to her left, while a few smart ones calmly wandered along behind to gather up what the others had left. Finally Sarah noticed us and waddled over. Yes, it was a waddle. We got out, and I watched as Diane gracefully walked around to the front of the car. She definitely did not waddle. Sarah came over and leaned up against the car, tilting it under her weight.

"You two don't look any worse for the wear. Barton must not have taken a shot at you."

"He did, but fortunately he missed," I answered. "But we got him to talk to us."

"Which one? The fat one or the tall one?"

"You knew that there were two of them?"

"Sure. Didn't you?'

"I just didn't think you knew."

"I figured you being the mailman and all, you'd know. So what did they tell you? They see anything that morning?"

"Well, yes. I don't know how to say this."

I found myself unable to finish my statement. Diane finished it for me.

"They said they saw you out there that morning."

"They did?" Sarah said, after an uncomfortable pause. Her face expressed more confusion than anger. "I don't see how they could have. I wasn't there. Haven't been for years."

"Why would they say something like that?" Diane asked.

"Barton even described the clothes you were wearing," I added.

Diane appeared a bit confused as Sarah's lips closed tight and quivered slightly. She turned away and looked across her farm. Finally she could not hold back any longer.

"Yes. I was there that morning. But when I got there, the doors were locked and I couldn't get in. And they weren't in the barn or in the fields."

"How come you never said anything about this to me before?" I asked.

"Afraid, I guess. And I really don't know anything more than you do. I didn't see anyone else out there. I thought it was better if I just stayed out of it entirely. Just leave me out of it."

Sarah turned and went back to her chores leaving

"So, do you believe her?" Diane asked.

"I believe what she told us. I just don't think she told us all she knows," I answered.

"What makes you say that?"

"You get to know a person and you get to know how they are. There was just something different today. She was holding something back."

"But what? Why?"

"She probably doesn't even know she's doing it."

Chapter 25

As the sun set, I looked out across the cornfields from my house. So peaceful. Yet it wasn't.

I walked over to my dresser and pulled open the bottom drawer. Lifting up three pair of torn jeans, I dug out the locked gun case. I searched through my keys and until I found the one that fit the lock and reluctantly opened it. Hidden inside was the 357 Magnum. The 357 Magnum I swore I would never use again.

I relived each day in some way each passing second. Yet I tried not to think of it in the next second. I couldn't get rid of the memories. I had bought the gun for my protection. After all, the crime rate in my city neighborhood had been on the rise for the previous ten years. Then, when my neighbor had been surprised in the middle of the night by an unwelcome intruder, I decided to acquire some protection of my own. I had considered various models of guns. Small revolvers. Pistols of many shapes and sizes. Guns that would slow down an intruder but not likely to cause any permanent damage unless a vital area was hit. I decided on the 357 for a couple of reasons. First of all, I didn't want to have to use the gun. A 357 might be intimidating enough that a would-be attacker might be scared away. Secondly, if I did have to use the gun, I didn't want the person to be in any position to defend himself in any way and maybe even use my gun on me.

When I first got the gun, I took lessons from a retired police officer who had been the most respected on the force. I spent many hours at the firing range taking target practice and got my license. I got to be quite proficient in the use of the weapon.

The night it happened I had gone to bed early. The 357 was on the nightstand next to my bed. Since I lived alone, I felt no need to keep the gun locked in my gun case when I was at home.

The first unusual sound woke me. The normal sounds— sirens, screams, cars without mufflers, slamming doors— those didn't wake me. The creaking of the stairs did. I sat up in the bed and listened. I could hear footsteps approaching the bedroom door. Without turning on the light, I reached for the 357. When I heard the doorknob turning, I aimed the gun toward the door. Suddenly, the bedroom door opened and I could almost see the intruder in dim light from the street lamp. I pulled the trigger.

Nothing happened. I had forgotten to load the gun. Just then the bedroom lights came on. I squinted in the bright light. I could just make out that it was my new girlfriend, Cheryl. At the sight of the gun, she turned quickly and ran out the door, screaming. That was the last I saw of her. And the last time I had touched a gun.

Chapter 26

Sarah was gone. I didn't know what to make of it. I hadn't expected Sarah to disappear. She was the stable influence in my life, the one thing that wouldn't change. Not only had I just found out that she might have been at the Novacek farm the day they had been killed, now she was probably gone for good.

"No, she didn't say where she was going. She said just to take care of things until she got back, so I'm taking care of things." With that said, Liz Kreyer quickly turned on her heels, and went back to tend to Sarah's chickens.

"So what now?" Diane asked.

I looked up toward the house. It stood mysteriously and oddly dark in the early evening dusk.

"I say we check out the house," I answered as I moved toward the front porch.

The door creaked open to an eerily silent house. No smell of baking bread or frying chicken emanated from the kitchen. The house, which was usually more than neatly kept, was now in somewhat a state of disarray. Diane entered first, tripping on a pair of overshoes that lay uncharacteristically in the middle of the entryway. I followed behind, catching Diane before she fell. My God, she felt good in my arms. It was as if she belonged there. Maybe she did, I thought. She slowly disentangled herself from my arms, smoothing her short skirt over her shapely legs.

"Nice save," she said. "Didn't think I was that clumsy."

No, I thought. She was anything but clumsy. I only wished she were more so. I could easily get used to catching her each time she fell.

I reached back for the light switch and turned on the lights. Now that the room was brightly illuminated, the room appeared to be even more of a mess. It wasn't as if the room was ransacked, just like it had been occupied by a bunch of teenagers for a few hours.

"This doesn't look right," I said as I cautiously made my way into the living room.

"What was your first clue?" Diane asked as she picked up a pair of boxer shorts and held it up and away from her between the two long nails of her thumb and forefinger. "Unless these are yours."

"Not mine, I don't wear 'em."

"Oh, so you're a jockey shorts kind of guy," she said as she dropped the boxers with one hand and suppressed a laugh with the other.

"You should know that," I said. A blush suddenly covered my face.

Diane moved slowly toward me, licking her lips and looking seductively toward my crotch.

"Prove it," she demanded, as she reached for the buckle of my belt.

For some reason, I shyly backed away.

"I already did. The day we went swimming at your uncles' place."

"I wasn't looking," she said as she moved toward me again. "What kind of girl do you think I am?"

I moved forward and put my arms around her slim waist. She looked up at me with her big blue eyes as I bent down to kiss her. That's when a loud bang resounded throughout the house, originating from upstairs. I reluctantly pulled myself from Diane and leapt up the stairs, Diane at my heels. I checked out the bathroom and a spare bedroom and found nothing strange in either room. Diane searched the attic with the same results. Together we entered Sarah's bedroom. There we saw the source of our rude interruption. A window had been left opened. A curtain tossed by the wind had knocked a vase off a nightstand and to the floor, where it lay in useless pieces.

"Sarah must be planning to come back soon," I said as I picked up the broken vase and tossed it into a wastebasket next to Sarah's bed. "Else she wouldn't have left her window open like this. Plus she left her pictures, television, tape player, and clock radio."

"I'm not so sure." I turned to see Diane standing next to an open closet door. She lifted her arm and clanged the empty hangers together. "She took all her clothes from here. How about the dresser drawers?"

I checked each drawer. As I had expected, each drawer was empty. I slowly closed the last drawer and walked to the bed and sat down.

"This doesn't make any sense at all."

"Not to me either," Diane agreed as she sat on the bed next to me. "Unless she actually did kill my uncles and now she's running away."

"I can't believe that!" I shouted angrily, clenching my fists and pounding them on the bed. And then more quietly, "I just can't believe that."

She looked into my eyes. Slowly her face moved closer to mine, her lips brushing against mine ever so slightly, causing a shiver to pass through me. As she moved away, she shivered too, as though the shiver had moved from me to her.

I studied her as she got up from the bed, wanting to hold her back, wanting to throw her on the bed, wanting to make love to her as I'd wanted to since the first time I had seen her naked in Sarah's bathroom.

Diane moved away from my outstretched hand and over to the window. The sunlight glistened off her tanned skin, her moist skin. My god, I thought! She's sweating! I knew what that meant! And unlike when I perspired, it was a good thing.

I started to move off the bed toward her, but she stopped me.

"Lean back on the bed," she said sensuously.

She moved over to the dresser and searched through some cassette tapes.

Finding one she approved of, she placed it in the tape player and hit the start button. When I heard the first notes, I recognized it as a song I had heard many times on the radio and at every wedding I had attended here. The Blue Skirt Waltz. An old-time polka band favorite.

Slowly she began to remove her blouse in time to the music. It was the most erotic strip tease I had ever seen. I would never be able to listen to the song in the same way again. Her skirt and bra removed and her back to me, she slid her panties to the floor and turned to me just as the song ended. She joined me on the bed

"Now it's your turn."

I got up to do my version of the strip tease. Fortunately the next song was the Beer Barrel Polka. My dance lasted about ten seconds.

Chapter 27

I was surprised to find a message from Ma Doherty waiting for me when I stopped home for a shower and change of clothes. I listened to it while I began to prepare a quick meal of Kraft macaroni and cheese. She wanted me to meet her at St. Scholastica Catholic Church Sunday, tomorrow, at one o'clock. A strange time and place, I thought. That was the extent of the message. Rather, it was more of a command. As if she had no doubt I would do as she wished. She was probably used to everyone, not only her sons, following her orders explicitly.

As I doctored the bland macaroni and cheese with some hot peppers, I wondered how she had gotten my phone number. I hadn't told her my name, and even if she had found that out, my phone number was unlisted.

My meal tasted better than I had expected. Perhaps the fact I hadn't eaten for the last twenty-four hours had something to do with it. In all that had happened since I had found Nick and Ted murdered, food had not been high on my list of priorities. Neither had sleep. I could barely keep my eyes open. I settled on the couch with a bottle of Stroh's and turned on the Twins versus Detroit. I was asleep before Kirby Puckett came to bat in the bottom of the first.

I awoke with the full bottle of beer still gripped tightly in my right hand, television still on, and the sun shining through the still-torn curtains. Reverend Schuler was preaching his energetic sermon, which meant it had to be at least eight o'clock in the morning. Since I was going to church, I decided to shower, shave, and put on a suit.

By the time I reached Little Chicago it was almost eleven o'clock. The rain shower I had met halfway to Little Chicago had stopped just a mile before town. As I passed the sign marking the city limits, I could see a mass of people surrounding the church. I was greeted by a teenage boy who waved me into a large sunken field which served as a parking lot. When I refused to obey his orders, he waved more vigorously. When I firmly held my ground, he angrily marched up to my car and demanded that I open my window.

"You're holding up the line," he shouted.

I looked behind me at the line that wasn't there. And then I again surveyed the parking area, which more closely resembled a swamp.

"I'm not going down there," I answered. "Those people can get stuck if they want to. But it doesn't mean I have to."

"You got to," he yelled. "It's the rules."

"You mean it's the rule I have to get stuck?"

This time it was he who firmly held his ground.

"Listen," I pleaded. "I'm Martin Prescott, here to see Ma Doherty."

"Ma Doherty! Why didn't you say so? She's at the church. You get to park up by the rectory."

I couldn't see the rectory, so I drove in the general direction of the church. A crowd of people blocking my path to the church miraculously parted like the Red Sea as I slowly made my way down the street. They closed in behind me, leaving me completely enveloped in the eye of the storm.

I found the rectory and parked my car in the last open parking spot. When I got out of the car, I saw Ma Doherty with one of the "tractor pull" thugs from Dillinger's near the entrance to the church. The church bells abruptly started ringing. She tossed a cigarette to the ground and stamped it out with her foot. When they headed through the church doors, I decided to follow them inside.

The interior of the church resembled the turn-of-the-century Catholic churches I had attended as a child: the stained-glass windows, the altar situated at the back of the sanctuary, and the pulpit towering above the congregation. The parishioners even recited the rosary in Latin.

When I took a seat in the last pew, all heads turned toward me. Gradually, the rosary died out. I could hear whispering behind me. I turned to see a line to the confessional. I got up and moved to a pew near the middle of the church. This must have made everyone more comfortable because the recitation of the rosary resumed.

I could see Ma Doherty in the front row. The priest emerged from the sacristy accompanied by the "tractor pull" thug wearing undersized altar boy's vestments. I would have to sit through a Mass before I found out what Ma Doherty wanted.

A family of four moved into the pew ahead of me, a father, mother, and two teenage daughters, aged about sixteen and fourteen. The women, as required, covered their heads. The mother wore a lace doily; the oldest daughter had draped a handkerchief loosely over her blond hair. But the youngest must have forgotten her doily at home since she wore a paper napkin from a fast-food restaurant attached to her hair with a bobby pin.

The Mass began, unusual these days in that it was conducted in Latin. I was amazed that I still could remember most of it. But, since I had gone to Mass seven days a week for eight years while in a Catholic elementary school, it shouldn't have surprised me. I even found myself confidently responding in Latin at each appropriate point in the service.

I also found my eyes riveted upon the napkin. Just after the Offertory, the father bent down and whispered something to the mother. She shook her head no, turned and whispered to the oldest daughter. After shaking her head no, she then relayed the message to the youngest daughter, whose first reaction was one of puzzlement. Finally, she shrugged her shoulders, reached up and tore the napkin in half and, leaving half in place on her head, gave the other half to her sister. She, in turn, handed it to her mother, who then handed it to her husband, who then used it to blow his nose.

When I looked up, I saw Ma Doherty was no longer in the church. Where had she gone? I exited the church to find her but she had disappeared.

The sound of accordions and drums filled the air. I followed the crowd toward the music. The smell of hot dogs, hamburgers, popcorn, and cotton candy got stronger as the music got louder. Hay wagons situated at various points throughout the church grounds served as stages for the bands, which, amazingly, performed simultaneously. People surrounded each wagon, some listening, some dancing. The dancers slipped and sloshed in the rain-drenched grass as mud covered their feet and legs up to their knees. An occasional dancer would fall, adding to his enjoyment as well as to that of the observers.

Three priests stood stoically next to the church. One quite elderly priest stared solemnly out into the throng, probably contemplating the state his churchyard would be in the next day. The other two, in their twenties, gazed enviably at the celebrants, as if they wished they could be a part of it themselves.

I walked up to the triumvirate. I was surprised to see a beer in each of their hands. The elderly priest stuck a cigar in his mouth, while the two younger ones each took a drag on cigarettes. As I passed them, I asked where I might find Ma Doherty. After looking me up and down closely, they pointed to a huge tent.

Bingo. That's what they were playing. And Ma Doherty was calling out the numbers. She was in charge. There was no doubt about that. As I walked down the center aisle of the smoke-filled tent, Ma Doherty called out a number.

"This here's your next number. O-92."

She looked up to see if any of the players were searching their cards for the number.

"And if you've got that one, you've got to be cheating. Either that or it's a miracle, because there ain't any such number."

She then called out the correct number. A woman aged about seventy croaked out a barely audible "BINGO."

"If you're foolish enough to throw away your cards now, it's you're own damn fault if she doesn't have bingo and you lose," Ma Doherty announced. "You should know as well as me, Emma don't know how to play this game. Emma, this better be a real bingo or we're going to start charging you double for wasting our time."

An attendant picked up Emma's card and rattled off the numbers and surprisingly Emma did have a real winner.

"Well," Ma Doherty said through a hoarse laugh. "Even a blind squirrel finds nuts once in a while."

I sat in a chair away from the smoke and waited anxiously. About midway through the next game, she spotted me and abruptly got up from her chair.

"You all can just take a break now," she announced. "I've got some business to take care of here and we'll start where we left off in about ten minutes."

Surprisingly, there were no groans or complaints of any kind. People seemed to accept it as a matter of course. Ma Doherty ambled toward me with a wry smile on her face. She stopped half way and pulled a pint bottle from her purse and took a healthy swig. When she reached me, she offered the bottle to me, which I refused as politely as I could. Even this small refusal on my part seemed to bother her. I could tell she was not used to being told no.

"You're early. Better than late, I always say," she said.

"You made it sound important."

"Damn right, it's important," she replied earnestly. "I got to thinking about what you said the other night. About my boys and your friends that got themselves killed. So I talked to them about it. And guess what?"

"They said they didn't kill Nick and Ted," I answered.

"Be quiet, now. I wasn't saying it as a question," she explained. "My boys didn't even know those Novaceks. They never even met them. What do you have to say to that?"

"I heard they did."

"There you go again. Talking when you should just be listening."

I just put my hand over my mouth and nodded my head. Talking to Ma Doherty had rules which I had never learned before.

"But," she continued. "My boys did say they've spent some time in Castle Rock. Said they've even played poker there a time or two. Guess who with?"

This time I knew better and waited for her to continue.

"Well, aren't you going to guess?"

"The Novaceks?"

"Here. I'll let them tell you themselves. They've been wanting to meet you. I've told them all about you."

She guided me into the church basement, past a line of women waiting to use what must have been the only ladies' room on the grounds. The rich smell of country cooking greeted me: mashed potatoes, gravy, turkey, ham, apple pie. People sat at tables gorging themselves as an army of waiters and waitresses hurried to keep up to their demands.

Ma Doherty led me to the kitchen where a group of heavy-set ladies in aprons slaved over hot stoves preparing the food as fast as they could, just barely keeping up with the demand.

"My boys are back in here," Ma Doherty said with a slight laugh.

Five skinny young kids ranging from about eighteen to twenty-three worked feverishly over a hot sink. These were her boys, I thought to myself.

"These are my boys," she announced proudly. "Don't be afraid of them. They won't bite."

Why anyone would be afraid of them was beyond me.

"Now tell him, Larry. Who was you was playing poker with?"

Larry stuttered the answer as quickly as he could. "Bud Helmsley, and Earl and some big fat guy named Ike."

The other brothers nodded in affirmation until Ma gave them a stern look. They quickly went back to their appointed tasks.

"What about the Novaceks?" I asked.

"Who the hell are they?"

"Two old farmers. A fat one and a skinny one."

"Them? All they did was sit and watch. And try to keep Bud from losing money. Not that they could stop Bud anyway."

"So when was the last time you saw Bud and the Novaceks?"

114

"That's easy," said Larry. "That was the night before they died. We left them. They were all headed to the old farmers' place. Bud was so drunk he passed out and had to sleep on the back seat."

Chapter 28

The Crow Bar was enjoying its usual Happy Hour. Unlike the upscale bars in the Twin Cities, the Crow Bar did not need hors d'oeuvres or even half-price drinks to lure its customers in after work. Just the ability to serve them drinks after a hard day's work was enough to attract them. That, and the fact that "everyone" would be there also might have had something to do with it. When I entered, I saw that all the old-timers held their usual stations along the bar, smoke hanging in a cloud in the air above them. The younger crowd occupied their usual booths and tables near the video games and pool tables. Euchre games were in progress in the back room, the retired men spitting into coffee cans and speaking in languages that I couldn't understand. The conversation died for a few seconds when I opened the door, and all eyes turned to analyze me before returning to the more important things they were doing.

Sheriff Trout and his men were nowhere in sight and neither was Ike, which left a big gap at the bar. No one bothered to occupy those spaces since they'd just have to move when Trout and Ike did arrive. Besides, they had their own places anyway. But it didn't stop me.

My eyes became more adjusted to the darkness of the bar after the brightness of the afternoon sunlight outside. Ella Masta, sixty years old but looking more like forty, sat on Tom Larson's lap in the corner booth. Tom was twenty and had just graduated from high school recently. They'd been seeing each other for five years now, as everyone will now finally admit. But the man I was searching for, Bud Helmsley, was not in the bar.

Roy, the bartender, mistaking me for Trout since I was occupying Trout's seat, poured a pitcher of Grain Belt and placed it in front of me. Not expecting any money he just turned and walked away. He stopped suddenly and turned back to me.

"You ain't Trout," he said,

"Glad you could tell the difference."

"Now that Earl ain't here, what am I suppose to do with this?" he asked as he pointed to the pitcher. "Don't suppose you want it, do you?"

"Maybe, if you answer some questions for me."

Roy grimaced as he shook his head. He never talked about anybody. In fact, the less he knew about a person, the better he liked it. He adhered to the belief that if people just minded their own business, there would be fewer problems in the world, and especially in the Crow Bar.

"What is it you want to know?"

"Have you seen Bud Helmsley?" I asked, as Roy turned to walk away. "Do you know where he is?"

"No idea," he answered as he busied himself with washing some glasses. "I haven't seen him since yesterday."

"I stopped by his house and it looked deserted."

"Doesn't surprise me," he stated.

"It doesn't?"

"No. After thirty years behind this bar, nothing surprises me anymore."

George Linch impatiently pounded his glass on the bar for another beer, drawing Roy away from me.

Just then, bright sunlight streamed into the bar as the door opened. The two long legs silhouetted in the doorway could only belong to one person. Diane. She entered the bar, followed by another figure, whose body blocked the sun. The door closed to reveal Ike as he placed his chubby hand on Diane's bottom and guided her to the booth occupied by a group of teenagers. He waved them out of the booth with his other chubby arm.

"This is our booth," one of the youths uttered.

"It's reserved," growled Ike as he forcibly removed the objector from the booth.

Diane entered the booth first, and Ike squeezed in next to her. I didn't think he could fit in there alone as well as have somebody in there with him.

It irked me, to say the least. What was she doing with Ike? I casually strolled over to their booth. At first, neither of them seemed to notice I was there, or let on that they noticed. Finally, Ike looked up and growled.

"What are you doin' here looking like one of Mary's lost little shepherds?"

"I just wanted a word with Diane."

"Diane? I don't know any Diane," he answered, looking over toward Diane. "Do you?"

"No, I don't know any Diane," she responded. With that she let out a derogatory laugh and looked at me like I was a complete idiot.

"See, there's no Diane here," Ike agreed.

"Don't give me that. You know damn well she's Diane."

Ike said, "If you mean Electra here, you're wrong. As usual."

"Electra! She's Diane!"

Ike gave a disgruntled look toward Diane.

"Okay, show him your ID. He won't believe me for some reason."

Diane pulled her driver's license from her wallet and slid it across the table toward me. Her picture was on it. But the name said Electra. Electra Kraus.

"But Sarah said you were Diane."

"Sarah was easy to fool. Not as easy as you. But easy enough."

Chapter 29

During the long drive back home, I tried to plan my next move. A beautiful sunset had turned into a gentle mist, and now was a steady rain. Sarah was gone. Bud Helmsley was gone. Diane was no longer Diane but Electra Kraus. That bothered me the most.

Bud Helmsley had been with the Novaceks' the night before they were killed and probably had been the last to see them alive, according to what I had found out at Little Chicago. I had to find out where Bud had gone. So I decided to go over to Bud's house to see if there might be some clue as to where he was.

When I arrived at Bud's, it was dark, and the steady rain had turned into a heavy downpour. The water flowing to the storm sewers was backed up over the curbs. As I opened my car door, a sheet of cold water splashed onto me, thoroughly drenching me in seconds. I stepped out into rushing water, soaking my shoes and socks. I began to wonder what I was doing out there. I could have been sitting in front of a warm stove with a beer in my hand. But I wanted to find Bud. I slogged on through the heavy rain toward the dark house, which was barely visible. Even though I was completely waterlogged, I ran toward the front door trying to avoid the raindrops.

When I reached the protection of the porch, I could hear the cloudburst pounding on the roof. I looked under the doormat and above the door for a key. Not finding one, I checked under some potted plants. The prospect of going out in the rain again to look for a partially open window to crawl through did not appeal to me. On a whim, I tried the front door. It wasn't locked. I was really getting good at this business of "breaking" into houses. I groped for a light switch and found it in what I thought was the wrong place. I flipped the switch and lights came on, showing the interior of Bud's house to be in the same shape as Sarah's. Someone left in a hurry, taking only the necessities.

I began my search of the house, checking the notepad next to the telephone. I took a pencil and gently drew back and forth over the paper, darkening the page, waiting for the phone number of the last person called to magically appear on the page. All I got was a darkened sheet of paper. It must only work in the movies. The search of the rest of the house produced the same non-results. I really didn't know what I was looking for. After all I was a mailman, not a detective.

A mailman! That was it. It wasn't something that was there that made me curious, but something that *wasn't* there. Bud had been gone for a few days now, but there was no mail inside the house by the mail slot. And I knew yesterday was the day Bud should have received his retirement check, a check that arrived punctually on the first Monday of the month. He must have forwarded his mail. I knew where to go from here.

Chapter 30

I was out in the rain again, this time, outside the post office doors. There was no porch to protect me this time. I had to hope Ike hadn't changed the locks. Why is it always the last key that works? Once inside, I used my flashlight to find my way through the halls. Everyone had gone home for the night and the building was dark, but I knew exactly where to go. I made my way to Mike Sandau's office. He was in charge of entering the change-of-address data. One day, when he had to go to his daughter's grade school play, he had taught me how to sign on to his computer and enter the changes for him.

I powered up the PC and waited for the prompt. I entered his user ID and it prompted me for his password. I could only hope that Mike hadn't changed it from his daughter's name Heidi. Heidi worked once I spelled it right. I searched for Bud Helmsley's name. The address where Bud Helmsley had forwarded his mail appeared on the screen. I wrote it down on scrap of paper.

I heard the front door open and close and footsteps march down the hall toward me. This time I wasn't going anywhere. If I was caught, I was caught. The footsteps stopped at the door to Mike's office. The light clicked on. There stood Diane. Or was it Electra? I wasn't sure.

"Did you get it?" she asked.

"Get what?"

"You know, where Bud Helmsley is getting his mail. Why else would you be here? You must have thought of it when I did."

"Or maybe you followed me here," I answered as my fingers moved swiftly over the keyboard, making changes to Bud's forwarding street address, city and state. "And if I did find it, why would I tell you?"

"Because we're partners, remember?"

"We were partners. That was before you suddenly transformed into Electra Kraus. Before you got attached at the hip to Ike."

I hit the enter key as Diane moved toward me. These changes to his address would be enough to throw them off. There would be a change record stored on the database but they would have no reason to check that.

"You're partners with Ike now," I continued.

"Oh that. That was just an act. I'm just trying to get on the good side of Ike," she answered. She stood behind me, pressing her body against the back of my head. God, she felt good. "We're still working together."

"So what have you found out from Ike?"

"Nothing. At least not yet. But soon. I can feel it."

So could I, as her breasts brushed against my head, causing a shiver to run up my back. Maybe I was wrong. Maybe she was putting one over on Ike. But maybe she was putting one over on me?

"So what did you find out?" Ike's voice interrupted. I looked up to see Ike filling the doorway.

"You almost had me fooled again," I shouted as I pushed Diane away.

"I've got it," Diane said to Ike. "We know where Bud is now."

Together, Ike and Diane rushed out the door, turning off the lights, leaving me in the dark.

Chapter 31

I was on my own again. I didn't have to worry about trusting someone, and I liked it that way. I knew I could trust myself, most of the time, at least when I wasn't under the influence of Diane. Diane just confused me. I could be sure the sky was blue until Diane was around, and then she could convince me it was plaid.

I was on my way to Duluth, a several-hour drive north on Interstate 35 from Minneapolis/St. Paul. Duluth was a beautiful city built on the hills that overlooked Lake Superior. In my younger days, I had spent many nights in the bars near the harbor. They were usually filled with sailors on leave from the many ore ships that stopped in Duluth. The men and women who frequented these bars were there primarily to drink and secondarily for more drinking. I had been there for the same reason. It helped me forget about my divorce. But I also felt like I belonged there. I must have, because I got into as many fights as everyone else did.

I arrived in Duluth at about midnight and I had no trouble finding Bud's address. It was an old mansion in a seedy area on North Shore Drive that had been converted to apartments. A chain link fence guarded the entrance to the liquor store across the street. The exterior of the bar next door needed painting.

Weeds brushed my pants as I walked up the steps to the darkened house. When I opened the front door, I expected to find a lighted entryway. But it was almost pitch black. I groped for a light switch and, not finding one, searched my pockets for a match or lighter. Being a former smoker, I was out of luck. Another reason to start smoking again. I felt a door on my left. My hands found a protruding nail and what appeared to be a number. Doing my best impression of reading Braille, I decided the number had to be a two. Since there was only one other door on this floor, I deduced that apartment #3 had to be upstairs and across the hall.

I slowly made my way up the dark stairway, almost tripping a few times on objects on the steps. I felt my way to apartment #3 and knocked on the door. The door was not completely closed and swung open. The light of the neon sign from the bar next door temporarily lit the room, blinking on and off. I tried the light switch. Nothing happened. I turned it on and off several times thinking that would help. It didn't. For some reason all the electricity to this apartment building had been turned off.

Whenever the reddish light illuminated the room, I moved a step further into the room. With each step, I encountered overturned furniture and papers on the floor. Someone had ransacked the place. Then I came across something soft but immovable. In the next reddish light, I saw Sarah, covered in red blood, made even redder from the neon light. I reached down and felt for a pulse. There was none.

I fled the apartment and rushed to my car. I reached under the seat for the bottle of Jack Daniels reserved for times like this. Like for whenever I found my fourth dead body in two weeks. Poor Sarah. Sheriff Trout was right. This finding dead bodies was becoming a habit with me. I was beginning to feel like Jessica Fletcher of "Murder She Wrote" or one of the Harts in "Hart to Hart." Wherever I would go, there would be a murder. People would stop inviting me places, or, they would leave whenever I'd enter the room, knowing that if I was around, a murder was sure to follow. Even if I wasn't a murderer, people would be killed just so I would discover the body. I took one good swig and planned my next move.

What was that they always said? Whoever they were. The killers always return to the scene of the crime. I started my car and moved it to the parking lot of the bar, next to the apartment building. I backed into an open spot where I would have a good view of the front door of the apartment, where I could see anyone coming or going. From inside the bar, I could hear the resounding beat of country music. Hank Williams Senior. "Window Shopping." One of my favorites that I rarely heard anymore.

An hour passed, with nothing happening at the apartment building. Patrons of the bar came and went. Some noticed me and gave me strange looks. Others ignored me. A particularly noisy couple left the bar. She was in her thirties, with blonde hair and a great figure, but her face had lost its beauty ten years ago. The man was in his forties, overweight, and balding. He was trying to get his hands on her as much as she was trying to keep them off her. For some reason they decided to perform this little wrestling match right in front of my car, leaning against the left front fender. Also, this put them directly between the apartment building entrance and myself, blocking my view. As they would make a move to the left, I would lean to the right. I felt like I was watching a tennis match. This went on for about five minutes. Finally, one of his giant meat hooks of a hand made its way up her skirt as she unsuccessfully attempted to move away.

For some reason, they had been totally unaware of my presence until that moment. They both stopped what they were doing and stared at me for a few seconds.

"Whatcha lookin' at, pervert!" the man shouted as the woman modestly tried to cover herself. The man moved toward my driver's window. I quickly locked my door and rolled up the window, accidentally hitting the light switch, horn, and turn signals in my haste. He reached for my door handle and tried to open it, rocking the car back and forth violently. After a minute of that, it finally occurred to him that the door was locked. The profanities flowed from his lips as his fists slammed against the windows. All this time, his blonde companion had been ignoring him and was now talking to a tall, much younger man in front of my car. It was when the two of them began to wander off to another corner of the parking lot that the car beater diverted his attention elsewhere and zigzagged away from my car.

That was when I noticed Diane walking away from the apartment building. Ike was nowhere to be seen. I had no idea whether she had been in the building the whole time and was now leaving, or had gone in while I'd been distracted. Maybe she had not gone in the apartment building at all.

She crossed the street and got into her car, which could have been parked there since I had first arrived without me noticing it. As she pulled out of the parking spot, I could see she was alone in the car. I decided to follow her. Just as I was about to turn out of the lot, a group of people leaving the bar blocked my path. By the time I was able to move, I had lost sight of Diane's car. There would be no way to trail her, so I backed my car into its former spot and resumed my watch.

After about a half an hour of watching drunks wander to their cars, the bar was about to close. I was ready to give it up. Two women, a tall, slim brunette and a short, chunkier blonde walking arm in arm exited the bar and noticed me. Giggling, they sauntered over and leaned their heads into my window. The taller of the two said they were headed for her place together and were wondering if I would be interested in a threesome. Reluctantly, I turned them down.

From behind the apartment building, I heard the creaking of a door being opened. From out of a run-down garage emerged two figures. The one in front was being pushed along by someone directly behind him. When they got into the light, I could see that the first figure was Bud Helmsley. As they went down the walk, I saw that the pusher was Diane's father, Lester.

When they got across the street, Lester forced Bud Helmsley into a car. Lester got in on the driver's side and started down the street. As I started my own car and began to leave the parking lot, I heard sirens and saw flashing red lights to my left. I had just about reached the street when the police converged on the scene, blocking my exit. They ran from their cars and entered the apartment building, leaving me stranded in the parking lot. Car chases were a lot easier in the movies.

Chapter 32

I woke up in my car in the same parking lot I had been in the night before. The last thing I remembered was watching the police put the yellow crime scene ribbon around the apartment building. That had been about three o'clock in the morning and my car had not been the only one in the lot. One car had contained a couple making out and three others sat vacant, their owners apparently having left them for the night. A dilapidated Ford pickup appeared to be a permanent fixture in the lot.

Now as the sun rose over the edge of Lake Superior, only the car that had contained the lovebirds was gone. But a few other cars had appeared.

At the apartment house, policemen and investigators entered and exited like bees swarming around a hive. Onlookers stood on the sidewalk behind the yellow tape, while a news crew interviewed the police chief. The detectives were probably searching the apartment for clues. My fingerprints were at the crime scene, I realized, since I'd felt my way around the around the apartment in the dark. It wouldn't take long before I would be implicated in Sarah's murder.

The passenger door of my car opened, taking me by surprise. The two legs I saw could belong to only one person. Diane. She gracefully slid onto the passenger seat. She smiled as she looked at me. It really was difficult not to smile back.

"What are you doing here?" I asked.

"Same thing as you," she answered.

"You better tell me then, because I have no idea."

She didn't or couldn't answer but turned away from me to stare at the apartment. Policemen were searching the grounds. Police dogs sniffed behind bushes and trees.

"I saw you there last night," I continued.

"I was, but it was dark and I couldn't get in."

"I was surprised I didn't see Ike also."

"Oh, him. I sent him on a wild goose chase to that phony address you gave us."

"How did you know it was phony?"

"I checked it out. There is no such address. Of course, Ike didn't bother to check. He just stupidly went there. I went back to the post office and got the real address from Ike's assistant, Mike."

"Why would he give you that?"

"Oh, he's seen me around Ike a lot. I just told him Ike needed the previous address. And if he didn't get it for me, Ike wouldn't be too happy with him."

"So I suppose you're going to tell me you aren't working with Ike. Again."

"I'm not," she answered. Looking at her eyes, I had a difficult time not believing her.

"Why should I trust you? He could be waiting in the car around the corner."

"He could be. But he's not. I'm not working with him. I was trying to tell you that before but he walked in on us at the post office. So I had to pretend to be working with him. I was trying to get some information from him."

"And did you succeed?"

"Yes. But I'm afraid I found out more than I wanted to know."

Already, I was falling for it, starting to believe her. There was that old saying: Fool me once, shame on you; Fool me twice, shame on me. I wondered if the next line was: Fool me thrice, I must like it.

"What was it you found?" I asked. "Or can't you tell me, Diane? Or maybe I should say, Electra?"

"It's Diane," she answered. She opened her purse and pulled the fake ID card from her wallet. "Look at it," she said, handing the ID to me.

I examined it closely. Her picture was on the ID but it appeared to have been tampered with.

"You see it's a fake. I had it made when I was underage and wanted to get into bars. Not a very good fake, but good enough to get me past bouncers in dimly lit entryways. I have no idea who this Electra Kraus is."

"So what information did you find out, Diane?" I asked as I handed the card back to her.

"It has to do with my father."

"What about your father?"

"I found out why my father was gone all those years. He was in prison. There was a bank robbery in Milwaukee where over a million dollars was stolen. A bank teller and a customer were shot and killed during the robbery. My father was arrested and found guilty. That's why my father was in prison so long."

"And now when he gets out," I said, "your uncles, Earl, and Sarah are mysteriously murdered. The thing is, you would think in a small town like Castle Rock, everyone would have known your dad was in prison."

"No, because it happened after my mother and I moved to Milwaukee. About the only people who knew about it were my uncles, Sarah, Ike, and Sheriff Trout."

"Diane, I saw your father here last night. It looked like he had a gun on Bud Helmsley, forced him into a car, and drove off."

"So my father is doing this," Diane said. "Even though I hardly know him, it's hard for me to believe my father is a murderer."

She moved over to me and nuzzled herself in my arms.

"It's hard to believe that about anyone," I said, comforting her.

I looked up toward the apartment entrance. Sarah's body, in a body bag, was being carried out on a stretcher. The curiosity seekers and the media moved in to get a closer look.

"Why?" I asked. "Why was Sarah killed?"

"Maybe she knew too much," Diane answered.

"Well, the answer isn't here," I said. "And if I'm right, it's in that farmhouse. And so are your father and Bud Helmsley."

"Well, we better check it out," Diane said excitedly, sitting up in the passenger's seat.

"We? Maybe I should do this on my own," I said.

"You still don't trust me."

"Well, do you blame me?"

"I guess not," she answered. "But either way I'm following you out to my uncles' farm."

Chapter 33

We headed back to Castle Rock. Diane followed in her red Corvette. I kept expecting her to pass my old beater, a 1973 Olds Cutlass. If she did, I would never be able to keep up to her. As it was, I could barely maintain the maximum speed limit of 55 miles per hour. I was embarrassed that my oil burner emitted an ugly dark cloud in her path so that I could barely see her car in my rear view mirror.

Just after sunset, we got to the Novacek farmhouse. We stopped at the end of the driveway and turned our head-lights off.

We got out to take a look. It was too dark to see if any cars were parked near the house, but in the living room, lights and shadows could be seen, as if someone were moving about with a flashlight or lantern.

We left our cars at the end of the driveway and made our way on foot to the farmhouse. We walked arm in arm to keep each other from tripping on ruts along the way. In another circumstance, it would have been quite romantic. The only sound in the night was of our heavy breathing. The crickets and frogs must have taken the night off. When we reached the house, we crouched down below the living room window. Along the ground, we could see shadows in the light from the window above. I took a chance at a peek in the window, and through the curtains was able to see dark shapes moving about. Diane pointed toward the back of the house.

Together we carefully made our way along the side of the house, avoiding the bushes and the propane gas tank. When we turned the corner to the back of the house, a bright light flashed into my eyes. A large hand gripped my shoulder, throwing me to the ground. My eyes adjusting, I made out the form of Ike towering over me, a shotgun pointed at me.

"I got him here like you wanted," Diane said. "Worked just like you said it would."

"Nice job," Ike answered.

Not again! How could I let myself be tricked again? Why don't they just shoot me and get it over with? It's what I deserved for falling for it again.

"Everyone else here?" Diane asked.

"In the house. There's some rope by the steps. Get it and tie him up while I hold the gun on him. Then we find out what to do with him."

Diane disappeared into the darkness behind Ike. I wished that I could do the same. Just disappear. I looked around for something, anything that I could use as a weapon. There was nothing. All I saw was the ground. Then I remembered something else I had seen in the movies. Where the hero takes a fistful of dirt in his hand and tosses it in the eyes of his enemy, temporarily blinding him. Just enough to allow the hero to grab the gun. With my right hand, I tried to grab a fistful of dirt. It was packed down hard. I tried my left hand. I did find a pile of something that wasn't dirt but I guessed dog shit would work just as well. I realized I could get killed trying this but I figured they would kill me eventually anyway. With all my strength, I threw a handful at Ike. Not only was my aim bad, but the stuff dissipated before it got halfway to him.

"What the fuck!" Ike growled. "That was a stupid-ass thing to do!"

Almost in slow motion, I could see him moving the gun toward me. Then I heard a thunk, much like the sound of a wooden bat hitting a softball. The gun dropped from Ike's hands as he fell forward toward me. I rolled away just before his gigantic body hit the ground with a thud. I looked up to see Diane with a two-by-four in her hands. She tossed me the rope she had been holding.

"Quick! Tie him up!"

I tied his legs and hands together behind his back. I removed one of his shoes, and then the sock, which I stuffed in his mouth to keep him from warning the others.

"Nice touch," Diane said.

"Thanks. Thanks for saving me," I answered. "I thought. . . . You know."

"Yes, I know what you thought," she said.

She came over and kissed me full on the lips.

I bent down and picked up Ike's shotgun.

"Now let's see what's going on inside."

Chapter 34

I opened the porch door about an inch at a time and then squeezed through. Diane tiptoed in behind me and carefully closed the door. Even if we had made a noise, they would probably think it was Ike. But it was best to have the element of surprise on our side. I peeked into the dimly lit kitchen and could see no one. Dirty dishes, beer bottles, a bottle of Jack Daniels, and a Kentucky Fried Chicken carton littered the kitchen table. The door from the porch to the kitchen was not visible to the rest of the house so it seemed safe to enter. Again we slowly opened the door and both entered the kitchen, careful not to move too far into the room where we could be seen through the long hallway from the living room. We pressed ourselves against the door and listened.

"Be reasonable." That was Sheriff Trout's voice.

"I've been more than fuckin' reasonable." It was the voice of Diane's father, Lester.

I looked at Diane. Her eyes danced back and forth. She nodded her head. I didn't know what the hell she meant by that. Yes, it was her father? Yes, it was Trout in there? Yes, let's charge the living room? All of the above? She was sweating, drops of perspiration rolled down her cheeks. This time, I knew her sweat did not mean she was horny.

"Yes, what?" I mouthed.

"Let's do it," she mouthed back.

Sexy as that was, she probably meant we should check out the living room. We slowly edged our way along the wall until we reached the hallway. Taking a deep breath, I quickly poked my head around the corner, catching a narrow view of the living room. I couldn't see anyone. This time I nodded.

"Yes, what?" It was her turn to mouth.

I motioned for her to follow me. We crept along the hallway, stopping when I saw Lester from behind as he pointed a shotgun toward Bud Helmsley. Neither of them could see us. I put my hand up to stop Diane. She moved up close next to me to get a better view.

"I don't know anything about any damn money!" That was Bud Helmsley.

So it had been her father all along. Now he had brought Bud back here for some money. And Sheriff Trout and Ike were working with her father. But how would Bud Helmsley know about any money?

"I know fuckin' well you do. I'm giving you five seconds."

I didn't wait to hear the rest. There had been too many people killed. Even though I couldn't have done anything to stop those murders, I wished that I could have. There was something I could do to stop this one. So I did. I jumped from the hallway and flung myself toward Lester.

"No, Martin! Wait! Don't!" I heard Diane shout behind me. But it was too late. Lester started to turn back toward me. But I hit him with a tackle that my high school football coach, Guts Hewlet, would have been proud of. The gun flew to the ground in front of Sheriff Trout who stood with his arms up next to Bud.

It was when I landed on top of Lester that I realized that I might have miscalculated.

"Goddammit!" Lester growled.

As I wrestled with him, I saw Diane make a dash toward the gun. But Sheriff Trout was able to bend down somehow, and reach the gun before she got to it. I looked down to find the gun I had dropped when I tackled Lester. It was just beyond my left foot. I quickly reached for it.

"Don't do it, Prescott!" I looked up to see Sheriff Trout holding the gun on me.

"Goddammit. Just when I get the best of these assholes!" Lester glared at me.

"Shut up!" Trout snarled. He pointed toward Diane. "You. Get over there next to them."

As Diane walked she gave me a totally exasperated look. "Not my dad. Trout and Bud!"

"Why didn't you say something?" I asked. Bud Helmsley picked up the gun I dropped. We now had two shotguns pointed at the three of us.

"Well, Martin. You are some damn good after all." Trout laughed.

"Good for shit," Lester growled.

That's what I felt like. You would think one of these times I'd make the right move.

"So, what do we do with them, Trout?' Bud asked.

"We've killed four already. What's a couple more?"

We were backed up against the wall. Literally. As I leaned back I felt a sharp object in the small of my back. I looked up into the glare of the harsh living room light. It was the only light on in the room.

"You get Martin's girlfriend first. So Prescott won't miss the show." Trout grinned. "Then Prescott's mine."

I slowly moved a hand behind myself until it touched the switch. Now was as good a time as any.

I flipped the switch off and the room went black. I pushed Diane and Lester toward the hallway. Fire shot out of the shotgun as the thunder of the shotgun echoed throughout the room.

I felt a burning ache on my buttocks as we fell into the hallway. Diane and Lester must not have been hit, because they scrambled to their feet and ran down the hallway toward the kitchen with me following. Another shotgun blast shook the house and splattered against the hallway behind me as Bud or Trout followed our sounds. There was enough light outside to make out the window on the kitchen door. I saw it open and the silhouettes of Diane and Lester scurry on to the porch. I followed, slamming the door. Another shotgun blast tore apart the kitchen behind me.

Outside we jumped over a squirming Ike and darted behind the pump house.

"Where now?" Diane asked.

I heard footsteps on the porch. They would be outside in seconds.

"There's only one place we can go without them seeing. The barn," I whispered.

Trout and Bud stopped outside the porch, looking for us in all directions. Bud spotted Ike and grabbed Tout's arm.

"Hey! There's Ike! Looks like he's trying to tell us something!"

"Let's get outta here!" Diane whispered. "Ike knows where we went!"

"Wait!" I answered.

I reached down in the shadow of the pump house cast by the yard light. In the weeds, I was able to find a few golf ball-sized rocks. My first toss was over the house. A loud clank resounded from the other side of the house as the rock hit something metallic, maybe even have hit one of their cars. Bud and Trout stopped before getting to Ike, turned and ran back toward the noise. My second toss headed toward the yard light. This time a slight "thunk" could be heard as the rock hit something wooden in the direction of our cars. That was good. Bud and Trout would think we were headed out the driveway. I took one more shot at the yard light. The yard went black as the light bulb exploded, the shattered glass raining on the gravel below. Pure luck on my part; I probably could have tossed a hundred times and not hit it again.

We ran toward the barn, a black silhouette in the dark night. We moved quickly but slowly enough to avoid making too much noise. I hoped any noise we did make would be attributed to restless livestock. I looked back toward the house and saw the lights from two flashlights as Bud and Trout made their way out of the driveway toward the main road.

When we reached the barn, Diane started to open the door. A groan began to emanate from the hinges.

"There's no way we can open this without them hearing," Diane said.

"Out back," Lester said. "Here. The fence."

Diane leapt over the fence, a standing high jump with no part of her body touching the fence.

Lester crawled over next, his large stomach stopping him at the top. I planted a hand on his butt and forced him over. He landed on all fours on the other side. I had an easier time of it. I just opened the gate and walked in.

We crept along the side of the barn. I looked back toward the driveway. I saw flashlights as Bud and Trout headed from the house, toward us. I heard a noise next to me by the barn.

"Shit!" Diane hissed loudly. She had tripped and sat with her butt in the manure pile, half of her backside was covered in cow-shit. "Why didn't you warn me?"

After her dad and I helped her up, she futilely tried to wipe the manure from her pants, managing only to smear it in more.

"Come on! Let's move it!" I said, probably louder than I should have.

We carefully tiptoed along the cement-block foundation of the barn to the back door. It was already open.

Once inside, Lester asked, "Now what?"

"Don't know about you. But I'm losing these," Diane answered.

I couldn't see what she was doing but I heard two shoes drop to the floor, a zipper being pulled down and then the sound of her jeans sliding off. Her disrobing in the dark was more erotic than watching most women in the light.

"They'll find us if we stand around here," Diane said as she hopped up and down, putting her shoes back on.

"Up to the hay loft," I said.

"I ain't going up there!" Lester growled. "I'll take my chances out there." And he was gone.

"What do you think, Diane?" I asked. "Want to follow him?"

"I'm with you," she replied, brushing against me as she led the way up.

"I'll be up in a minute," I said. Then I picked up her jeans and ran out into the cow yard toward the pasture. About thirty yards from the barn, I tossed the jeans in the direction of the pasture and ran back to the barn and up to the loft. When I reached the dark haymow, I could smell the alfalfa bales. Pigeons cooed in the rafters, ruffling their feathers as they moved about above us.

"What now?" she whispered. "I can see them moving around the yard. They're bound to look up here sooner or later."

"Follow me."

I grabbed her hand and we climbed the stack of bales. Each layer up had one less bale, creating a stairway to the top. After reaching the top, we made our way to the back of the barn, occasionally stepping into the cracks between the bales. I heard the mumble of voices in the yard. I turned to see the two flashlights headed toward the barn.

I groped for a bale, finding one I pulled it from the top of the pile.

"Here," I whispered. "Let's make it harder for them to find us."

As she pulled the bales out, I stacked them against a far wall. The creak of the barn door opening echoed throughout the barn. I crawled back to Diane, who was now in a hole five bales deep. I joined her in the crevice, took the fifth bale, and balanced it on the next-to-top layer.

"Now all we can do is wait," I said.

Diane snuggled close to me, the cool skin of her bare legs rubbing against my sweating arms. I could hear someone climbing up the ladder. Two loud thumps sounded as Bud Helmsley stepped off the ladder into the hayloft.

"You don't think they were stupid enough to hide up here in the hay, do you?" he yelled down to Trout. "I'll smoke 'em out."

The sound of the shotgun blast filled the hayloft. The pellets splattered against the bales and against the barn wall just above us. I could hear Bud climbing up the bale staircase. When he reached the top, he shot another shell at the top of the stack.

"Hey, Bud!" Trout yelled. "Come on down here. I found her pants."

"Her pants?"

"Just her pants. Looks like Prescott and the girl are headed out to the pasture."

Bud ran down the stack of bales and down the ladder to join Trout.

"You okay?" I asked Diane.

"Yeah. And you?"

"Fine," I answered, as I felt something warm running down the side of my head. "Except I think my head's bleeding."

Chapter 35

I moved my hand to the blood running down my cheek. In the dark, Diane's hand touched the side of my face.

"Oh my God!" she said.

My heart skipped a beat. I feared the worst. Had she discovered a gaping hole in my skull?

"What is it?" I managed.

"If that's your blood, it's the slimiest I've ever felt."

I could hear her sniff her fingers, the sound louder in the dark.

"And your blood smells a lot like eggs."

"Eggs, you mean?"

"Yes, you weren't shot, just egged."

I suppressed a laugh. I could hear Diane trying to suppress a laugh of her own. She wasn't successful, as she burst out laughing. Then I joined her. If Trout and Bud were nearby, they would have heard us. But we couldn't stop. Whenever we were able to, one of us would start up again and then the other would join in. And it wasn't even that funny.

"But I think I'm bleeding," she whispered when we both had finally calmed down. "This alfalfa is scratching my bare legs all to hell."

Instinctively I reached down and felt her legs, the welts rippling beneath my fingertips.

"Ouch! That hurts!"

Being the gentleman I was, I started to remove my pants, just as I would offer my coat to a woman who was shivering in the cold night air.

144

"What the hell are you doing?"

"I'm giving you my pants."

"The hell you are!"

But I already had them off and was attempting to slip them over her feet. She resisted by kicking her legs. The harder I tried the more she kicked. Soon we were wrestling. That's when I noticed she was sweating. Was it a sweat from fear or exercise? Or was she getting horny? I had never seen her perspire from fear or exercise before. So I opted for the latter. I must have been right. When my mouth found hers, she kissed me as I had never been kissed before. Her hands reached under my shirt and pulled it over my head. My hands moved under her blouse and felt her small, firm breasts. Soon we were both naked. My body found hers and we made love. The alfalfa cut into our skin as we moved against the bales, the pain accentuating our pleasure. The fear of being discovered and killed made it ever more exciting. This was the second time I had made love to her and this was even stranger than the first time, but much more pleasurable than I thought possible.

Later we lay in each others' arms. I had no idea how much time had passed. Sometimes hours pass as minutes, and at other times minutes pass as hours.

"Now what?" she asked.

"We can't stay here all night," I answered. "Once it gets light, they'll have an easier time of finding us."

"I don't hear anything out there," she whispered. "I'll check to see if I can see them."

"No, let me."

"I can do it," she insisted.

"We'll both look. But first let's put on our clothes."

That was no easy task. It was difficult finding our clothes in the dark. I put on my tee shirt and then discovered I was attempting to put on Diane's panties. She convinced me that my pants would be too big for her. But she did accept my long sleeve shirt so she wouldn't be running around half-naked.

We tossed the bale from above us and crawled out. The smell of gunpowder filled the air. We moved toward the barn wall toward the pasture. Looking out the cracks, we could see Trout and Bud's flashlights not far off. We climbed down the hay bale staircase to the loft floor. The boards creaked below. Through a dirt-stained window we could see the house. The two lights were approaching the driveway toward the yard. When they reached the yard, they stopped and focused on the barnyard. If Bud and Trout came again to the barn now, they would surely hear us if we tried to make it back to our hay bale hideaway. I could hear them mumbling as they discussed their next move. Suddenly the lights turned toward the house. As they disappeared inside, Diane and I quietly made our way down the ladder. When we reached the barn door, we both had the same idea. We headed for the pasture.

"To the cars, right?" she asked after we had reached a safe distance from the house.

"Right. They've checked them already."

Quickly, we ran through the wooded pasture, stepping into cow pies and tripping on fallen branches. When we reached the fence, I could see our cars down the road. I pulled the barbwires apart for Diane to crawl through. She slipped through without touching a wire. Then she held the wires apart for me. I, however, was not as graceful and caught the back of my shirt. The barbs tore the shirt and into a good piece of my back. I flopped to the ground on the other side. Diane helped me up and we raced for the cars, the gravel crunching beneath our shoes.

"We'll take my car. It's closer," Diane said.

When we reached her car, Diane reached for the handle.

"Hold it right there!"

It was Ike. I'd forgotten about him. He again had a shotgun pointed at us.

"Trout figured you'd end up here. I should finish you both but he wants the fun of doing it himself. Now both of you head down the driveway toward the house."

Ike herded us down the driveway toward the house, the barrel of his gun poking me the back whenever I walked a little too slow. Diane moved ahead of me by about five yards.

"Slow down there, girlie," Ike growled. "I don't want you running off on me. Else I'll just have to shoot Prescott here in the back."

Diane waited for us and then fell into step next to me. It seemed like the driveway was a lot shorter as we rapidly approached the yard. I could see Trout and Bud moving about in the now well-lit farmhouse. In a few minutes, we would be in the house, where Trout would waste no time in eliminating us. The hero in a movie would turn quickly, surprise Ike, and wrestle the gun away from him, allowing the girl to escape. But I was no hero. Maybe there was a better way. I slowly veered off the driveway in a direct line toward the house, across the lawn.

"Where you headed, Prescott?"

"This is the shortest way to the house. Why go the long way? I just want to get this over with."

"What the hell. Why not?"

We trudged across the tall grass toward the front door, snaking our way around trees and shrubs. Then we came to the spot I was looking for. It was a narrow opening between two bushes. I stepped on some boards that lay in my path and guided Diane to the right of the two bushes. The boards sagged beneath me but manage to hold my weight. Ike followed me and stepped onto the platform. The boards groaned under his weight and, with a loud crack, gave way.

"What the . . .?" Ike yelled as he crashed though the platform, falling down the old well. I just hoped he would fit. At the same time, his gun went off, a bright blast of light shot out into the black night air. He landed with a loud thump at the bottom of the well, yelling and cursing.

I grabbed Diane's hand and pulled her back toward the end of the driveway. I looked back to see Trout and Bud running out of the house, flashlights in hand. We were about halfway down the driveway when they spotted us. We heard a gunshot as pellets hit the dirt behind us. Diane and I each had the same idea. We jumped into the tall weeds in the ditch. I followed her as she crawled along the ground toward our cars. The light from their flashlights against the weeds cast long shadows on the field next to the ditch.

We reached the end of the driveway and ran in a crouch toward our car.

"Hold it! Stop right there!" Trout shouted just before we reached our car.

"Don't shoot!" I yelled as we stopped and turned around, our hands in the air.

"The hell I won't!" he shouted back.

I heard the blast and cringed, but realized I hadn't been shot. I looked over toward Diane to see if she had been shot. We were both standing. Trout's flashlight crashed to the ground, leaving us in the dark. Bud aimed his light toward Trout, who lay there in a heap. Then Bud looked up at the shooter.

"Don't shoot!" Bud screamed, dropping his gun.

Lester moved into the circle of light with Trout. I had forgotten about him. He picked up Trout's flashlight and turned it on Bud, who lay on the ground in a fetal position, rocking and silently sobbing like a baby.

"It's over," Bud whimpered. "It's finally over."

Chapter 36

"We have to let someone know what happened," Diane said.

We were sipping beer and drinking shots of whiskey with Lester and Bud in the farmhouse. We had to contact the authorities but we weren't sure which. Who would believe us?

"But what *did* happen?" Lester asked. "Maybe Bud can tell us?"

Bud looked drained. His chin rested on his chest.

"No need for that," I said. "I figured it all out. Bud killed Ted and Nick."

Bud shook his head no.

"No. I guess it started with me. And the gambling. At first I won. I won a lot. I was going to be rich and do all the things I wanted to do. Travel. I was going to take Sarah with me. We were going to go to Europe and Hawaii and the South Pole. But then, I started losing. I knew it was only temporary. I'd win again. I had won before and I would again. But I didn't. I had to borrow money. Ike was happy to lend it to me. Pretty soon it was so much I could never pay it back. All of a sudden, Ike wanted his money. I told him I didn't have it. He said if I'd help him, he'd forgive the debt. What could I do? That night Trout, Ike, and I came out here, I didn't think anything would happen. We were just going to scare Nick and Ted. After all it wasn't their money. It was his."

Bud pointed to Lester.

"You see, Ike was always reading mail. He read a letter from Lester to Ted and Nick. It said Lester was getting out of prison and would be there to pick up his money. Trout and

Ike knew how much was stolen in the bank robbery he was involved in. Almost two million dollars. And it had never been recovered. Ike just knew that Ted and Nick were keeping it for him.

"That night we wanted that money. It wasn't Nick and Ted's money. It didn't belong to anybody. Might as well be ours. At first, they weren't going to give it to us. But after Ike pointed his gun at Nick, Ted said okay, he'd hand over the money. And he did. All $323 of it."

"All $323?" Lester said. "It was only $311! Money I made at the prison. I sent it to them for safekeeping."

"That's what Nick said, $311 plus interest. But Ike didn't believe him. And then he lost it. The two blasts went off just like that. And Ted and Nick were dead."

"So Ike made it look like a murder and suicide," I said.

"No, that was Trout's idea. He was furious. Said we'd never get the money with the brothers dead. But Ike said we could search the house later. We were bound to find it. But we didn't."

"So you figured I had it," I said. "That's why you ransacked my house!"

"No," Bud responded. "We were pretty sure if you had the money, you'd turn it in to Trout. We just wanted to scare you. Hoped you'd stop meddling in our business."

Diane asked, "But why kill Earl? He was just a harmless drunk."

"That's easy," I answered. "They caught him in the house, looking for the money."

"No. He heard us talking about the murders in the bar one day. I thought he was in the can but I turned around and he was right behind me drinking my beer. He said he wouldn't talk but Ike didn't trust him. We lured him out here on the premise of free beer. Ike just shot him and buried him under the rubble."

"What about Sarah? Why Sarah?" Lester asked.

"She found out and was going to talk, right?" I said.

"No. She knew about it from the beginning. But she wasn't going to talk. I knew that. Finally I had enough and Sarah and I took off. Where no one could find us. But Ike found us. In Duluth. Found her actually. I was out getting take-out from the Chinese Dragon. When I got back, she was dead. I knew I couldn't call the police. I was going to take off when Lester showed up."

"I saw him with a gun on you in Duluth. So why did he drag you back here?" I asked.

"He didn't," Bud answered. "I don't know what you think you saw but I got the gun on him and brought him back here. I figured he might know where the money was. The rest you already know. "

"You know, Martin," Diane chuckled. "You're not very good at this."

From outside we heard a loud moan that sounded like a cow giving birth to a calf.

"What the hell was that?" Lester asked.

"That's Ike! He's still in the well!" I exclaimed. I had forgotten about him.

Chapter 37

The sunlight peeked through the cracks in the blinds, creating a grate-like pattern on my bed. I looked over at Diane who lay sleeping peacefully at my side. It was the first night of normal sex we had had. The events of the last few weeks had taken their toll on each of us. Finally, it was at an end. Ike had finally confessed to everything. The fact that we wouldn't let him out of the well until he did confess might have had something to do with it. Bud had already told the whole story to Trout's Deputy, George.

Five people from Castle Rock had died. That was a lot for a community of five hundred people. That would be like killing four thousand people from Minneapolis in one month.

Most of the people from town no longer believed I had committed the murders. They had been lifelong friends of Trout and Ike and didn't think them capable of the crimes, but now blamed Bud for the whole series of events. Some people actually treated me like I was no longer an outsider. I had been offered Ike's old job at the post office and it was even suggested that I run for sheriff.

Diane awoke and smiled up at me. I never expected to be with someone so beautiful and intelligent. The sheet slipped down as she turned to me, exposing a seductive breast. With her at my side, my life was perfect. She kissed the nape of my neck, sending shivers up my back.

"Well, I guess I better get ready to go back."

That sent a cold chill throughout my body. Better get the rest of town back from hell.

"You're going?" I asked.

"I've got to. You know that. My whole life is there."

"But I won't go there," I said, sitting up in bed, folding my knees up into my arms. "I can't."

"That's right. You can't. You see," she wrapped the sheet around herself and swung her legs over the side of the bed, her back to me, "I'm engaged."

"Engaged?" I said as nausea hit me in a giant wave. "But? You and I?"

"You and I what?" she said gently. "We had sex. It was beautiful and passionate. But I have a fiancé and I cheated on him. I have to deal with that. I have to live with it."

"It's worse for me," I said. "I have to live with it, too. And without you. Why didn't you say something?"

"Selfish, I guess. I knew if I told you we'd be just friends." She turned back and smiled. "And I wanted more."

She got up from the bed, letting the sheet slip from her body. I couldn't resist watching as she dressed. Even watching her dress turned me on. I knew it would be the last time I would see her naked. Last night was the last time we would make love. I closed my eyes to fight back the tears. I felt her lips brush against my cheek. I still smelled her sweet smell after she left the room. I heard the front door close behind her. I jumped out of bed to see her drive out the driveway and maybe out of my life forever.

THE END